THE GUNSMITH

483

Belle Starr's Daughter

**Books by J.R. Roberts
(Robert J. Randisi)**

The Gunsmith series

Gunsmith Giant series

Lady Gunsmith series

Angel Eyes series

Tracker series

Mountain Jack Pike series

**COMING SOON!
The Gunsmith**
484 – To Steal from the Dead

For more information
visit: www.SpeakingVolumes.us

THE GUNSMITH

483

Belle Starr's Daughter

J.R. Roberts

SPEAKING VOLUMES, LLC
NAPLES, FLORIDA
2023

Belle Starr's Daughter

ISBN 978-1-64540-971-7

Chapter One

Clanton, Alabama

Clint Adams wasn't exactly sure how he came to be in Alabama. He hadn't been this far south since the Civil War. But tracking down a vicious killer, determined to bring him to justice for murders committed in Kansas, had brought him all the way here. Hopefully, Clanton was the last stop in a long hunt, as word had reached him that Del Thaxton was there.

When he rode into town on his Tobiano, they were both in need of rest and food. Although much of the town resembled many Western towns he had been in, there was still a definite Southern feeling to Clanton, one he had not experienced for a very long time. The Civil War years he had spent in the South were during his late teens and early twenties. Riding through Alabama had already reacquainted him with the people and the food. For the most part Southerners were good people, friendly. It was only when they realized he was a Northerner that some of them changed their attitudes.

As he rode into town, he kept a sharp eye out for Thaxton. It was entirely possible that the man didn't know Clint was on his trail, so there wouldn't be any reason he wouldn't walk the streets. When Clint spotted the livery stable he stopped, dismounted and walked Toby over to it.

"Help ya?" an old man asked. Clint assumed this was the hostler.

"I need to put my horse up," Clint said.

"How long didja have in mind?"

"I'm not sure," Clint said. "Could be a couple of days."

"Dollar a day do ya?"

"That's fine."

"I'll take 'im, then," the man said, reaching for the reins. "Fine lookin' animal."

"Thanks. Just let me get my rifle and saddlebags."

"You gonna be lookin' fer a hotel?" the man asked, while Clint removed his belongings from the saddle.

"I guess so."

"The Alabaman's the best," the hostler said. "It's toward the middle of town. You probably rode past it. And Lily Mae's Boarding House is good, too. Depends on what you want."

"Just looking for a room," Clint said. "Breakfast and a room."

"Well, then either one'll do ya," the man said. "Good rooms and fine vittles in both."

"Much obliged," Clint said. He started to leave, then turned back. "Any other strangers come to town lately?"

"Depends on whatya mean by lately," the man said.

"Last few days?"

"One or two," the man said. "You lookin' for some-one?"

Clint decided to keep that information to himself. At least, until he saw the sheriff.

"Nope," he said, "but I will need to talk to the sher-iff."

"That'd be Terry Poole," the hostler said. "The sher-iff's office shares a building with the post office. Ya can't miss it. If yer goin' to the Alabaman, it's right across the street."

"Much obliged."

"And if yer lookin' fer a good steak, try Muldoon's."

"Sounds Irish," Clint said.

"Sure is, but he's tryin' to get over it. The grub's pretty good."

"You got anything else to tell me?"

The man thought a moment, then said, "No, I think that's it. I'll see to your horse, now."

"Thanks."

Clint left the livery and started walking back the way he had ridden into town. He thought he remembered seeing the Alabaman Hotel and the post office.

When he reached the hotel, he saw the post office across the street. Under the sign that said, 'Post Office' was one that said, 'Sheriff's Office.' Under that, in smaller print, it said, 'Sheriff Poole.'

He decided to check into the hotel before seeing the sheriff and went into the lobby. The young woman behind the desk smiled at him—a very friendly, Southern smile.

"Can I help you?"

"Yes," Clint said. "I'd like a room."

"Of course," she said, reversing the register. "Please sign in."

He signed his name and wrote "Las Vegas, New Mexico" next to it.

"Do you have any idea how long you'll be staying?" she asked.

"Possibly a few days."

"Then I'll give you room six," she said. "It's our nicest."

"It doesn't overlook the street, does it?"

"No sir," she said. "It's very quiet and private." She held the key out to him.

He accepted the key and said, "Thank you. That sounds perfect."

She looked at his name in the book.

"If you're hungry, Mr. Adams, I think I can arrange something for you."

"That sounds perfect too, Miss . . ."

"Dexter," she said, "Julie Dexter. I should have something ready in about twenty minutes."

"Thanks," Clint said. "I'll be right down."

Chapter Two

Clint freshened up and came back down in nineteen minutes. Julie Dexter looked up from the desk and smiled.

"I have a snack ready for you in the dining room. You can go ahead."

"Thank you."

He walked across the small lobby to the dining area he saw when he first entered. He could see tables and chairs through the doorway. As he entered he noticed about eight tables. On one of them was a tray covered by a cloth. He walked to it, sat down and removed the cloth. A rather large sandwich sat on a plate. The meat looked like turkey or chicken, along with deep green lettuce and very red tomatoes.

"How does it look?" Julie asked, from the door.

"It looks great."

"Can I get you some water? Or coffee? We don't serve any alcohol here."

"Coffee would be great. Just black, and strong."

"Coming up."

He picked up the sandwich and bit into it. The meat was tender and the lettuce crisp. The tomatoes were sweet, and there was some kind of spread on the bread.

He had already taken several bites when Julie returned with the coffee. She poured a mug full for him and left the pot.

"Do you just work here, or do you own the place?" he asked.

"A bit of both," she said. "My mother owns it."

A quick scan of the register when he signed it told him that Del Thaxton had not signed in.

"What brings you to Clanton?" she asked. "It's such a small town."

"I haven't been in the South in a long time," he said. "I thought I'd see how things had changed since . . ."

"Since the war?"

He nodded.

"You fought for the North."

"I did," he said.

"You must have been very young."

"I was."

"I wasn't born yet, of course," she said. "But I've heard stories. Tell me, if you knew then what you know now, would you still have fought for the North?"

"I would, yes," he said. "Now you probably want your sandwich—and room—back."

"No, I don't," she said. "I don't hold it against you which side you fought on. The war was so long ago."

"I wish some other folks I've run into felt the same way," he said.

"The war will never be over for some people," she said. "I know a great many of them."

"Like your mother?"

"No," she said," my mother feels the same way I do. She was a child during the fighting. She says she doesn't remember much of what went on."

"That's possible."

"But you do?"

"I remember everything that happened," he told her.

"Maybe I should feel sorry for you," she said. "Anyway, what do you think of what you've seen of the South?"

"It's very beautiful," he said.

"I'm told it was even more beautiful before the war," she said.

"I'm sure it was."

Clint remembered seeing scorched ground and burnt-out buildings. Sometimes, right after the war, he would dream about the damage they had all—Union and Confederate soldiers—done. Even now, twenty years later, he had seen some signs of it as he rode through.

"I have to go back to the desk," Julie said. "When you're finished you can just leave everything here. I'll clean it up."

"Thank you for this," he said, gesturing with the remainder of the sandwich. "It's very good."

"You're welcome," she said and left the dining room.

Chapter Three

Clint's next move was to cross the street and meet Sheriff Poole. When he reached the door he decided, since he was in the well-mannered South, to knock.

"Come in," a deep bass called out.

Clint opened the door and entered. From the sound of the voice, he expected a large, barrel-chested man behind the badge. Instead, he was a small, grey-haired man in his fifties sitting behind a desk.

"Sheriff Poole?" he asked.

"That's right," Poole said. "What can I do for you?"

"My name's Clint Adams."

Poole frowned.

"Adams, the Gunsmith?"

"That's right."

"What's a legend of the West doin' down here in the South?" Poole asked.

"I trailed a man here."

"To my town?"

"That's right."

"What's he done?"

"Well, he killed several people during a bank hold-up," Clint said.

"I don't see you wearin' a badge, Mr. Adams," Poole said. "

"No, sir, I'm not."

"Have you turned bounty hunter, then?"

"No."

"Then why are you huntin' this man?"

"One of the people he killed was a friend of mine," Clint said. "I swore to him on his death bed that I'd find Del Thaxton and bring him to justice."

"By killin' him?" Poole asked.

"That'd be up to Thaxton," Clint said. "I'd rather bring him back to Kansas alive and put him on trial."

"Kansas?" Poole said. "You have come a long way, haven't you."

"Yes, I have."

"And you want my help?"

"No, sir," Clint said. "I'm only here to tell you I'm in your town, and I'm not looking for trouble."

"Is this fella Thaxton gonna be hard to take?"

"He won't go peacefully," Clint said, "but I'll do what I can to take him."

"Alive."

"Yes, alive," Clint replied. "As I told you, that's my preference."

"But if he resists?"

"I'll take him any way I can," Clint said. "But I don't want any innocent bystanders getting caught in a crossfire."

"That's good to hear." Poole stood and Clint thought the man would probably top out at five-seven. The lawman stuck out his hand and Clint shook it. "Thanks for comin' to see me, Mr. Adams. I hope this comes out the way you want it to."

"So do I, Sheriff," Clint said. "So do I."

Poole walked Clint to the door.

"Where are you stayin'?" he asked.

"Across the street at the Alabaman."

"Best place in town," Poole said. "Too bad you can't just enjoy your stay."

Clint opened the door and stepped out.

"One more thing," Poole said.

"What's that?" Clint turned and asked.

"When you catch him, I suspect you're gonna want to put him in my jail."

"I suppose you're right," Clint said. "But it would only be overnight. Once I catch him, I'm going to want to head right back."

"All right, then," Poole said. "I think we're on the same page."

"I think we are, Sheriff," Clint said. "I think we are."

Chapter Four

Clint returned to the Alabaman, which had a large, curved front porch. He chose one of the several chairs and sat facing the street. He spent a few hours just relaxing, watching the people walk by. He was hoping he would see Thaxton, at some point, but it didn't happen that afternoon.

As it came close to dinnertime, more people started to walk past him to enter the hotel. They all looked at him curiously, and some of them nodded. He assumed they were going in to eat in the dining room. Many of them passed past him again as they left, looking satisfied with their meals.

He saw Julie come out the front door. When she saw him, she walked over.

"Mind if I join you?" she asked.

"Don't you need to be behind the desk?"

"My shift is over."

"Then be my guest."

Clint was sitting on a wooden chair, but the one Julie pulled over next to him was wicker.

"I like to do this, too," she told him, "Sit out here and watch the town go by. Do you do this everywhere you go?"

"I'll usually spend some time just sitting and watching," he told her. "Especially if it's a pretty view."

"When you're looking for someone in particular?" she asked.

He looked at her and asked, "Is that a guess?"

"No," she admitted. "My mother looked at the register and recognized your name. She says you're a famous gunfighter."

"I don't see myself as a gunfighter," he said.

"She says there are books written about you," Julie said. "Are they made up?"

"Mostly, yeah," he said. "No one has ever written my real story."

"Why not let somebody do it?"

"I'd have to talk," he said, "a lot. There's plenty I don't want to talk about."

"So no one's ever done an interview with you?"

"I've never agreed to an interview," he said. "Even if I did, I don't think it would be presented accurately. Newspapermen tend to . . ."

"Lie?"

"Embellish."

"Well, I think my mom's afraid you're going to end up shooting up our lobby," Julie said. "I told her she's being foolish."

"Thanks for that," he said.

"I think it might be a good idea for me to introduce you two," Julie said.

"At some point that would probably be a good idea."

"Sure," she said, "we could do it later."

They sat in silence for a while, and then she asked, "Are you going to come inside for dinner?"

"I will," he said, "but I've noticed people coming and going. Your dining room must get crowded."

"People don't mind waiting in the lobby for a table to open up. We try to accommodate everyone who comes in." Julie got to her feet. "I'll make sure there's a table for you."

"Thank you," he said. "I'll be in presently."

"No hurry," Julie said, "but my mother is behind the desk now. I'll be in the dining room."

"I'll come and see you," he promised. "Make sure your mother knows I don't intend to shoot up the lobby."

"I will," she said. "See you later."

She turned and went back into the hotel.

Clint wondered if the word was getting out that he was in town. Thaxton might hear it, but there was no reason the killer would know Clint was hunting him. He might be expecting someone, but not the Gunsmith. He would be looking over his shoulder for a lawman.

He stood up and went inside for dinner.

Chapter Five

The dining room was small, but Julie had managed to isolate one table for Clint. When he appeared in the doorway she came over to him.

"I thought you'd want a table away from the others," she said.

"Actually," he replied, "what this'll do is make me stand out even more."

"Oh!" she said, looking upset. "I'm sorry. I thought—"

"It's fine, Julie," he said. "I doubt the word has spread on me, this soon."

"Not from us," she assured him. "We haven't told anyone you're stayin' here."

"The only one I've told is Sheriff Poole," he said, "and I doubt he's told anyone."

"Then you'll sit?"

He smiled at her and said, "Lead the way."

He followed her across the small room, attracting looks from some of the other diners.

"Do you want to see a menu?" she asked him.

"Surprise me," he replied.

"I will."

She gave him a big smile and went to the kitchen.

Crossing the lobby to the dining room, Clint had glanced over at the desk. The woman behind it appeared to be in her thirties, an older version of Julie. He assumed it was her mother, a lovely woman who showed what the pretty young girl would look like when she got older. The woman looked at him briefly, at the gun on his hip, then turned away.

When Julie returned, she was carrying a large plate with steam rising from it.

"You look like a steak man to me," she said, setting the plate down in front of him.

"You're exactly right," he said. The hunk of meat on the plate looked to be approximately thirty-two ounces, surrounded by potatoes and carrots, covered with onions.

"Can I get you a beer to go with it?" she asked.

"That'd be perfect."

"I'll also bring a basket of hot biscuits," she promised, and hurried off.

But he was surprised when it wasn't Julie who returned with the beer and biscuits, but her mother.

"Here you go," she said, putting them down.

"Thank you," he said.

"Do you mind if I sit for a moment?" she asked.

"Not at all."

She sat and stared at him,

"I know who you are, Mr. Adams," she said. "I recognized your name in the register."

"Julie told me."

"My daughter is very impressionable," she went on.

"I don't mean to—" he started, but she cut him off.

"Please," she said, "just let me have my say."

"Of course."

"And please, continue eating," she said. "Don't let it get cold."

"Of course."

As he cut into his steak, she continued.

"I don't know why you're in town," she said. "Hopefully, you'll do what you came to do and leave. But while you're here I don't want you to turn my daughter's head. She's eighteen and, as I said, impressionable."

"She seems pretty intelligent and level-headed to me," he commented.

"Under normal circumstances, yes, she is," the woman said. "But it's not every day a young girl gets to meet a legend like the Gunsmith."

"Miss—" he started, then stopped and started again. "Mrs. . . .?

"Mrs. Dexter is fine," she said.

"Mrs. Dexter, I'm not here to impress your daughter. But she's been very nice to me, so I guess you could say she's impressed me."

"Please," she said, sounding alarmed, "she's very young. You could turn her head very easily."

"I don't have any intention of turning her head. I fully intend to do what I came here to do and be on my way, as soon as possible."

"That's good to hear." She stood up. "Please, enjoy the rest of your meal."

He said, "Thank yo—" but she walked away.

Clint turned his full attention back to his meal, which was excellent. He was almost finished when Julie put in another appearance. By this time all the other ta-bles were empty.

"What did my mother want?" she asked.

"She didn't tell you?"

Julie shook her head.

"She just said she wanted to bring you the biscuits and beer. But I knew she wanted to talk to you. What was it about?"

"Basically, it was about one thing."

"And what was that?"

He looked her in the eye and said, "You."

Chapter Six

"About what?"

"I think she's afraid I'll play with your emotions," Clint said.

"You mean she thinks you'll make me fall in love with you?" Julie asked.

"Well—"

"Ewww," she said. "No offense, Mr. Adams, but you're a little old for me."

"Then we all agree on something," he said.

"I mean, I'm interested in you," she went on, "and the way you live, but I'm not foolish enough to think there could ever be anythin' between us. I mean . . . ewww."

"Yeah, okay," Clint said. "I get it." He picked up his beer glass and finished it off. "By the way, who cooked the steak, you or your mother?"

"Oh, neither of us can cook," she said. "But we have someone who can. His name's Ernie, and he can cook anythin'."

"Well, give Ernie my compliments," Clint said. "That was possibly the best steak I've ever had."

"And you've had a lot of steaks, I'm sure," she said. "I'll tell 'im."

He stood up and walked out to the lobby with her.

"I have work to do," she told him.

"I'll see you around, then."

"See you."

Clint saw her mother keeping a sharp eye on them from behind the desk as they split up.

***

With not much daylight left, Clint went back to the porch and sat. There was little chance in his mind that Thaxton would walk by, but he needed time to figure out his next move. If Thaxton was staying in town, he would need to be staying in a hotel or rooming house. Maybe the next morning he would try Lily Mae's that the hostler told him about. Thaxton probably wouldn't want to sign a hotel register.

He remained on the porch til late before going to his room and turning in. It had been a tiring day.

***

The next morning Rosie Lee Reed woke to a ruckus downstairs. She got out of bed, put on a robe, and went to see what the problem was.

When she got downstairs, she realized somebody was pounding on the front door. One of the girls, a little blonde named Goldie, was standing with her back pressed up against it.

"What's goin' on?" Rosie asked.

"Oh, a couple of men won't take my word for it that we're not open yet."

The pounding continued and a man's voice shouted, "Come on, come on, let us in!"

Another voice added, "We got money."

"I'll handle it," Rosie said. She generally had the confidence to handle any situation. She had much more maturity than most nineteen-year-olds, which was how she had come to own The Doll House, a whorehouse that featured young girls.

"Are you sure?" Goldie asked.

"Go on, get some breakfast."

"All right."

As Goldie went toward the kitchen, Rosie went to the door with one hand in her robe pocket.

She opened the door and two burly men stepped back in surprise.

"Hey, it's about time," one said. "Let us in."

"We're not open yet, gents," Rosie said. "Go get yourselves some breakfast and come back after noon."

"But we're ready now," one man said.

"We got money," seemed to be the only thing the other one could say.

"I'll be glad to take your money," Rosie told them, "but later."

"Come on, girlie," the first man said, "let us talk to your mother."

"My mother?"

"Or whoever owns this joint."

"I happen to own it."

"You?" the man asked. "Ain't you a little young for that? There must be somebody older in charge."

"I'm afraid not," she said. "I'm in charge, and you boys have to go."

"Now wait jus' a minute—" the man said, grabbing her left arm. Luckily, it was her right hand that was in her pocket. She brought it out and pointed a little derringer at him.

"Let go!" she ordered.

The man did, but as he did, he laughed.

"Hey, Mokey, lookit the little toy gun."

The other man, Mokey, also laughed.

"Whatchoo gonna do with that toy, little lady?" the first man asked.

"I'm goin to put a thirty-two-caliber hole in you if you don't turn around and walk away."

"You'd kill me just for grabbin' your arm?"

"I'll put a hole in your knees for not walkin' away," she said. "The choice is yours."

"If we walk away, you really think we'd come back after you pointed your toy gun at us?" he asked.

"Frankly," she said, "I don't care if you ever come back."

She stepped back inside and slammed the door. She stood with the gun in her hand until she was sure they had gone, then put it back in her pocket and went to the kitchen to see what was for breakfast.

Chapter Seven

When Rosie entered the kitchen, Goldie was seated at the table with two other girls. They all had plates overflowing with bacon-and-eggs. At the stove, cooking, was Charlie Moon. He had long, black hair, held off his face by a red bandana. The muscles in his arm looked like big, round, solid rocks. He was a member of the Northeast Alabama Cherokee tribe.

"Charlie," she scolded, "I've told you not to feed these girls so well. You're going to plump them up."

"You want' them to be too skinny," he said. "The women of my tribe were not plump, but they were healthy. I want these girls to be healthy. Now sit down and I'll feed you."

Rosie sat.

Charlie brought her a heaping plate of eggs and said, "Goldie says there was trouble at the front door. Why didn't you call me to handle it?"

"I handled it myself, Charlie," she said. "I can handle most situations myself, you know."

"I know you think that, Rosie," he said, "but I'm here to take care of things like that."

"I know, Charlie," she said, "and when there's somethin' I can't handle, I'll call you."

Charlie wanted to argue, but two more girls came into the kitchen, so he went back to the stove. None of the five girls sitting at the table with her were over twenty-one, except Ella who was twenty-two. The others all called her 'the old lady.'

"Goldie, you're finished with your breakfast. Go wake the other girls."

"Sure, Rosie."

The little blonde rushed from the kitchen.

"You sure got her trained," one of the girls said.

Before Rosie could answer, Charlie Moon said, "You should all learn to obey the way she does. Rosie is the boss."

"Come on," the girl said. "Admit it. Charlie's the boss and you're fronting for him, right?"

"Wrong!" Charlie said. "This is Rosie's place."

"How could that be?" the girl asked. "You're so young. I mean, you're my age."

"My mother left me some money and I bought this place," Rosie said. "Simple as that."

"That's what you wanted to do with your inheritance?" the girl asked. "Buy a whorehouse?"

"It wasn't a whorehouse when I bought it," Rosie said, "but it is now. And you're one of my whores. Don't forget that. Now go get cleaned up and ready for work."

The girl started to say something, but saw Charlie Moon staring at her, so she got up and left the kitchen.

The other girls got up and one said, "We'll go get ready, too, boss."

When all the girls were gone Charlie sat across from Rosie and chewed on some bacon the girls had left on their plates.

"Don't you think these girls would be more obedient if you told them who your mother is?"

"It's nobody's business. Besides, what makes you think they'd believe me."

"I'd back you up," Charlie said.

"I still don't think they need to know," she said.

"Do you wonder where she is?"

"Since the death of Sam Starr, she's given up her bandit ways. No, I don't wonder where she is. I think she's probably in hidin'. Prison took a lot out of her."

"Don't judge her too hard, Rosie," Charlie said. "She had a tough life."

"That makes two of us," Rosie said. "All she ever did for me was give me the money to buy this place. I'm makin' the most of it." She stood up. "I'm gonna get dressed for the day. I have to go out to do some shopping."

"I'll go with you."

"No," she said, "you stay here and watch over the girls. I don't know if those two yahoos will be comin' back."

"Take the buckboard."

"I'm not shoppin' for anythin' heavy," she said. "I'll be back in a couple of hours."

"One minute longer and I'll come lookin' for you," he warned her.

"You worry too much, Charlie."

He picked up a bunch of plates from the table and said, "Sometimes I don't think I worry enough."

Rosie smiled at him and went to her room to dress.

***

Clint rose early and had breakfast in the hotel's small dining room.

"Not a very busy, morning," he said to Julie as she brought him his food.

"We do a good business for dinner, but not much for breakfast."

"What about lunch?"

"We close for lunch so we can get ready for dinner. Enjoy your breakfast."

Clint did that, then walked out to the porch. As he got there, he was surprised to see a girl about Julie's age walking by.

"What's wrong, Mr. Adams? You look like you've seen a ghost."

Julie had come out of the hotel at that moment and was standing by him.

"Who's that girl, Julie? Do you know?"

Julie looked where he was pointing.

"Oh, everybody in town knows that girl," she said. "Her name's Rosie Lee Reed."

"She lives here in town?"

"On the edge," Julie said. "She has a business there."

"What kind of business?"

"She runs a whorehouse."

Clint looked at Julie.

"She runs it?"

"Runs it, owns it," Julie said. "She's the madam."

"The ma—how old is she?"

"My age," Julie said. "Nineteen."

At nineteen, Rosie looked just like her mother did at that age.

Her mother was Belle Starr.

Chapter Eight

The two men banging on the door of The Doll House that morning were Lou Hanley and Buzz Windham. They had been sent to do some damage to the building and, if need be, to Rosie Reed. But she had surprised them by pulling the derringer.

As they walked away from the house, Windham said, "Now what? We can't go back and tell him what happened. He'll kill us."

"We don't have to go back," Hanley said. "We just have to wait."

It turned out they didn't have to wait very long. When Rosie Lee Reed came out, they followed her at a safe distance. When she went into the General Store, they knew their time had come. They positioned themselves on either side of the door.

***

Rosie Lee went into the General Store and approached the counter.

"Miss Reed," the clerk said.

"Otto," she said. "My order come in?"

"Oh, it's here. I wrapped it up, just like you said to."

"That's fine," she said. "I'll take it."

"Yes' Ma'am."

He reached beneath the counter and came out with the package. It was fairly light and fit right under Rosie's arm.

"Thank you," she said.

"No problem."

Since she had paid for the package in advance, she turned and walked out the door.

The clerk breathed a sigh of relief. He had promised Rosie that the package would arrive today and had desperately wanted to keep that promise. He was one of Rosie's best customers and didn't want his wife to find out. With the package in Rosie's hands, his secret was safe.

***

When Rosie came out the door each man grabbed an arm. Her package fell to the boardwalk. Hanley grabbed the drawstring purse she was carrying. He could tell from the weight that her little derringer was in it.

"What the—oh, you two?" Rosie spat.

"Yeah," Hanley said, "us."

"Give me my purse!" she yelled.

"We can't do that," Hanley said. "I can feel that your little toy is in here, and we don't want to go through that again."

"What do you want?" she demanded of the two burly men.

"Well," Hanley said, "we were supposed to bust up your place some this morning, but I guess we're gonna hafta settle for bustin' you up."

"Should I break her arms now, Lou?" Windham asked, with a big smile.

"Buzz, we're gonna bust both her arms," Hanley said, "and that's just for starters."

That made Windham laugh, but he stopped when he heard a voice.

***

Clint had continued to watch from the porch as the two men passed by, obviously following Rosie Reed.

"I'll see you later, Julie," he said, and sprang from the porch.

He followed after the two men, saw Rosie go into the General Store, and then the two men stand on either side of the door.

It was obvious what they were planning.

Chapter Nine

As the two men grabbed hold of Rosie Lee Reed, Clint moved in close enough to hear their words.

"Let the girl go!" he yelled. "Nobody's breaking anybody's arms."

The two men turned in the direction of the voice.

"This ain't none of your business, friend," Hanley said. "You'll move on if you wanna stay healthy."

"I'm making it my business," Clint said.

"This girl mean somethin' to ya?" Hanley said. "She's a whore, you know."

"She's a lady, and you're not treating her like one," Clint said.

Rosie didn't know who Clint was, but she was grateful for his intervention.

"Watch out for these two, Mister," she advised. "They're idiots."

"Watch it, girlie!" Windham snapped, squeezing her arm and making her cry out in pain.

"That's it," Clint said. "Let her go . . . now!"

"We'll let 'er go just long enough to take care of you, friend."

Both men released Rosie's arms and turned to squarely face Clint. They were on the boardwalk, and Clint was in the street, so they were looking down at him.

Hanley dropped Rosie's purse, and he and Buzz Windham both went for their guns.

Clint drew and fired twice, putting one bullet in each of their chests. Both men looked dumbfounded. They fell to the ground, their guns still in their holsters.

Rosie had made a dive for her purse, but the two men were dead before she could get her derringer out.

Clint stepped up and reached out a hand to help her to her feet.

"Are you all right?" he asked.

"Yes, I'm fine," she said, pushing her derringer back into her purse. "I've never seen anyone draw a gun that fast. Who are you?"

"I think we might have to deal with the sheriff first." He pointed at the lawman, who was rapidly approaching.

"I'll tell Sheriff Poole you saved my life," she said.

"Appreciate that."

He picked up her package and handed it to her.

"Thanks for that," Clint said.

"What the hell happened here, Adams?" Poole demanded, "Miss Reed?"

"These two men were going to kill me, Sheriff," Rosie said. "This gentleman saved my life."

"I'm gonna get these bodies off the street," Poole said, "and then I'll want to talk to both of you in my office."

"That's fine with me, Sheriff," Clint said. "I'll walk the lady over there."

"That'll be fine, Adams," the sheriff said. "I'll see you there presently."

"Come on," Clint said to Rosie.

***

As they entered the sheriff's office Clint said to her, "You should sit."

"I think I will."

She took the chair in front of the sheriff's desk. Clint sat behind it.

"The sheriff called you Adams," she said.

"That's right."

"The only Adams I can think of who could draw a gun that fast would be Clint Adams, the Gunsmith."

"Right again."

"What are you doing here?" she asked. "How did you know I was in trouble?"

"I'm staying at the Alabaman. I was sitting on the porch when I saw you walk by," he explained. "I recognized you and saw those two following you."

"Recognized me? We've never met."

"That's right," Clint said, "but you're the spitting image of your mother when I knew her."

"You know who my mother is?"

"Belle Starr, right?"

"That's right," Rosie said. "When did you know her?"

"During the war."

"You fought together?"

"Not together," he said, "but on the same side. How is she?"

"Fine, I guess. I haven't seen her in some time."

"I was told your name is Reed. You're using your father's name?"

"Yes. I don't want anyone hereabouts to know who my mother is."

"Why not?" he asked.

"Well," she replied, "as you can see, I can get into enough trouble on my own, without people knowing Belle Starr is my mother."

Chapter Ten

Clint realized that letting people know that Belle Starr was her mother would bring Rosie a lot of unwanted attention. Considering what had happened today, the young madam might have enough trouble on her hands, as it is.

"What did those two have against you?" Clint asked.

"Originally, I thought it was because I wouldn't let them in when they pounded on my door this morning. But it was more than that. They said they were sent to bust my place up, but they'd settle for busting me up, instead."

"Then somebody out there has something against you," Clint said.

"In spite of the fact that you saved me today, I can handle things myself," she told him. "I have an Indian friend named Charlie Moon helping me."

"Where was he today?"

"I told him to stay at the house and keep an eye on the girls," she said. "I didn't expect any trouble."

"Well," Clint said, "if you get more than you can handle, I should be in town for at least a couple more days."

"What are you doin' in town, anyway?" she asked.

"I'm tracking a man named Thaxton. He killed some people in Kansas, including a friend of mine."

"Do you have a badge?"

"No badge and I'm not after a bounty," Clint said. "I just want him."

"I don't know anybody by that name," Rosie said. "Give me his description and I'll talk with my girls."

"That's a good idea," Clint said. "Thanks."

But before he could say another word, the door opened and Sheriff Poole marched in.

"Do you mind?" he said to Clint.

"Not at all, Sheriff," Clint said, vacating the lawman's chair.

Poole sat behind his desk, looked at them and said, "Okay, I'm ready. What happened?"

Between them they related everything that occurred since Rosie stepped out of the General Store.

"Ben Griffin told the same story," Poole said when they were done.

"Ben Griffin?" Clint said.

"The owner of the General Store," Poole said. "He saw the whole thing."

"Then why did you need us to go through it?" Rosie asked.

"I needed to confirm the whole story," the lawman said.

"So then we can go?" Clint asked.

"Sure," Poole said. "It's obvious you saved Miss Reed's life. You can both go."

"Thanks a lot," Rosie said, and headed for the door.

"She might be a target, you know," Clint said. "Maybe somebody should watch her."

"Sure," Poole said, "why don't you do that?"

"I've got my own problems."

"That didn't stop you today."

"You don't think you should help her?"

"If she asked, I would."

"But you know she won't ask, don't you?"

"She's a stubborn little lady," Poole said.

"Yeah," Clint said, "I get that."

He left the office, found Rosie waiting for him outside.

"I just wanted to say thanks, again," she said.

"Would you like me to walk you home?" he asked.

"That won't be necessary," she said. "I'm sure I'll be fine."

"Keep that derringer handy," he advised.

"I usually do."

"You didn't today."

She turned red.

"They surprised me," she said, tightly. "It won't happen again."

"I hope not."

Without another word, she turned and stormed off.

***

Approaching the whorehouse, she immediately knew something was wrong. The front door was wide open. She put her package aside and took out her derringer.

When she reached the front door, she paused and listened. There were no sounds coming from inside.

"Charlie?" she called "Goldie?"

There was no reply. Then she heard running steps behind her. She turned and saw Ella coming toward her, with the middle-aged doctor trying to keep up.

"Ella! What happened?"

"I don't even know," she said. "They kicked in the front door and all hell broke loose."

"Where's Charlie?"

"He's inside. I ran for the doc."

"I better go in," Doctor Hicks said.

"You better let me go first, Doc," Rosie said.

"Whatever you say."

Keeping the derringer pointed ahead of her, she went through the door.

Chapter Eleven

"Goldie!"

"Here!"

The voice came from the sitting room. Rosie picked her way through shattered pieces of furniture. In the sitting room she found Goldie and the other girls. One single sofa was still right-side-up. Charlie Moon was lying on it. He looked dead. Several of the girls gathered around him had bruised faces, including Goldie.

"What happened?" she demanded, as the doctor rushed to Charlie's side.

Goldie stood up.

"There were five of them, Rosie." She said. "And it took all five of them to do this to Charlie."

"Is he alive?" Rosie asked.

"He's alive," the doctor said, "but he's badly hurt." The sawbones turned and looked at Rosie. "I'll need to get him to my surgery."

"Do you have men who can move him?" she asked. "Otherwise, me and my girls—"

"I'll get a few men and a buckboard," the doctor said, cutting her off. "Don't you try to move him. I'll be back as soon as I can."

"What can we do in the meantime?" Rosie asked.

Hicks shrugged and said, "Pray."

***

The doctor and three men struggled with Charlie Moon's dead weight, but they eventually got him out of the house and loaded onto the buckboard.

"We'll take him right to my office," the doctor said.

"I'll be behind you," Rosie told him. "Do any of my girls need to be treated?"

"It doesn't look like any of them are badly hurt," Doc Hicks said, "but if you want to bring them, I'll have a closer look.

As the buckboard pulled away Rosie went back inside, where the girls were waiting.

"Goldie, are you all right?" she asked.

"Just bruised."

"And the others?"

"The same," she replied. "Those men concentrated on Charlie, and then on smashing the furniture."

"All right," Rosie said, "I'm going to the doctor's office."

"What should we do?" Goldie asked.

"Send Ella for Hardy Silver, the carpenter. He'll fix what he can, starting with the front door."

"What if those men come back?" Goldie asked.

"I doubt they will, but break out the guns and give one to each girl. You've all had lessons."

"Yeah, but we ain't never shot at anyone," a girl named Debbie said.

"Well," Rosie said, "you may have to."

Carrying her derringer, Rosie headed for the doctor's office. Her wrapped package was still on the ground.

***

When the doctor came out of his surgery Rosie braced him.

"How is he?" she demanded.

"He might have a skull fracture," the doctor said. "If he does there's nothing I can really do. If he doesn't he should wake up, eventually."

"Does he have any other injuries?"

"I'm thinking some broken ribs, and his left arm is fractured."

"How long will it take him to wake up?" she asked.

"Like I said, it all depends on whether or not they fractured his skull. But he's a strong man and that might be his best chance."

"Can you keep him here?"

"Yes, I have some empty beds," the doctor said. "What about your girls?"

"Like you said, they're all bruised, but that's it."

"Miss Reed," Hicks said, "what will you do if these men come back?"

"We've got guns," Rosie said.

"Don't you think you better talk to the sheriff?" Hicks asked.

"You know Sheriff Poole, Doc," she said. "What do you think he'll do?"

"I know you're an independent young woman, Miss Reed," Hicks said, "but I think you need help. The girls told me there were five men."

"Yes, I know," Rosie said, and counting the two who had grabbed her in town, that made seven. Somebody was intent on doing her—and her business—some serious damage.

"You might be right, Doc," she said. "I might need help, and I think I know where to get it."

Chapter Twelve

When Clint left the sheriff's office, he briefly watched as Rosie walked away. When she was out of sight, he walked to his hotel.

As he entered the lobby Julie rushed from behind the front desk.

"There you are," she said. "I was worried. Where did you go?"

"I had to help a lady."

"Rosie Reed? A lady?"

"What would you call her?" Clint asked.

"She's . . . a girl."

"A girl with her own business," Clint said. "She's your age, Julie. Don't you consider yourself a lady?"

"Well, yes, but . . . I'm not a whore."

"Neither is Rosie."

"But . . . she runs whores."

"Yes," Clint said, "she's a madam, but not a whore. So that makes her a lady."

"So what help did she need?"

"A couple of men tried to harm her. I stopped them."

"How'd you do that?" When he didn't answer right away, she said, "Oh."

Clint looked past Julie and saw her mother come through a doorway and stare at them.

"I think your mother wants you."

Julie turned to look.

"I'm supposed to be behind the desk. Where are you going, now?"

"To my room for a bit," Clint said. "But then I'm going out again."

"To find that man?"

"Yes."

"Do you think you can?"

"I've come a long way," Clint said. "I'll do it."

"Julie!" her mother called.

"I have to go," Julie said, and rushed back to the desk.

Clint went to his room.

***

After cleaning up, he cleaned and reloaded his gun. If the two men he killed had friends—or partners—he would need it. He also took his Colt New Line out of his saddlebag and tucked it into his belt, at the small of his back. He had no idea how many friends they might have.

Before he could leave to begin his search in earnest, there was a knock at the door. He approached and opened it a crack. Standing in the hall was Julie's mother. He opened the door wide.

"Hello, Mrs.—"

"Just call me Helen," she said. "May I come in? I'd like to talk."

"Of course," he said. "It's your hotel. Or yours and your husband."

"I haven't had a husband for a very long time," she said, walking past him. She was wearing a shirt, trousers and boots.

"All right if I close the door?" he asked.

"Of course."

He closed it and turned to face her.

"You dress more for outdoors than indoors," he observed.

"I spent many years outdoors, until my husband died," she said. "When I took over the hotel, I maintained the same dress code."

"Two guns," she said, noticing his holstered Peacemaker and the New Line he had just finished cleaning. "You must be expecting trouble."

"I've already had some," he said, "but I'll try to keep any more away from your hotel."

"I'm more worried about Julie than I am the hotel," she said.

"I can assure you, Helen, I'm not going to put Julie in any danger."

Helen fixed him with a hard stare that, somehow, made her look even more beautiful. Julie had a lot to look forward to if she matured into another version of her mother.

"It's not even the physical danger I'm worried about," Helen said. "I'm afraid she's going to get hurt, emotionally."

"I hope you don't think I would try anything physical with your daughter," he said. "She's so young."

"I've read some of the books written about you, Mr. Adams," Helen said.

"If you've read some of those books you might as well call me Clint."

"Clint, you have almost as much of a reputation with Women as you do with guns."

"You can't believe everything you read," he told her.

"Nevertheless," she said, "I'd like to find out for myself."

"What are you saying?" he asked, frowning.

She started to unbutton her shirt. "I came here prepared to sleep with you."

"I don't have time—"

She peeled her shirt off, revealing herself to be naked underneath. Her bared breasts were breathtakingly rounded and pale, with large, pinkish nipples.

"I want to make sure you're not tempted by Julie." She sat on the bed and reached down to slide off her boots. Her breasts swayed in a mesmerizing manner,

"Helen, please—"

Next, she stood and slipped out of her trousers. Lastly, she dropped the wispy, silk thing covering her pubic patch to the floor and stepped out of it.

"Helen—"

She put her hands on her hips and said, "Now don't make me beg, Clint. I assume you won't be keeping those guns on during sex."

"I don't keep them on," he told her, "but they'll be close by."

"Whatever," she said, "Let's get to it. I'm sure we both have other things to do."

Staring at her naked form Clint's hands started to itch and she made his mouth water.

She watched closely as he removed his gunbelt, hung it on the bedpost, and set the New Line aside on the night table. Then he started to take off his clothes. He decided she wasn't allowing him any way around this, so the only thing to do was give her what she wanted,

And, at that point, it was what he wanted, too.

Chapter Thirteen

Downstairs, Julie was surprised to see Rosie Lee Reed enter the lobby.

"Can I help you?" she asked, as Rosie Lee reached the desk.

"I'm lookin' for Clint Adams," the young madam said.

Julie's mother told her she was going to Clint's room to talk with him and didn't want to be disturbed.

"I'm afraid he's not available, right now," Julie said. "Can I give him a message?"

Rosie made a face and said, "I suppose I have no choice. Just tell him I need to see him as soon as possible."

"Can I tell him what it's about?"

"I think he'll have a fair idea what I want," Rosie said.

"Then I'll give him the message."

"Thank you."

Rosie turned, walked away a few steps, then turned back and looked at Julie.

"You have a lovely place here," she said.

That surprised Julie, but she recovered and said, "Thank you very much."

Rosie turned and walked out.

***

Once he was naked Clint turned to Helen, took her into his arms and kissed her, their bodies pressed tightly together. She felt his solid column of flesh crushed between them, reached down to take hold of it with one hand. She squeezed it tightly while they continued to kiss, then abruptly stepped back so she could take hold of it with both hands.

"I think I see where your reputation comes from," she said.

"Not yet, you don't," he said.

He put his hands on her hips, turned her and pushed her back to the bed. She allowed him to push her down onto her back. From there he got on his knees, took her legs and put them on his shoulders. Her legs were spread open far enough for him to press his face to the sweet, wet lips of her vagina.

"Oh!" she yelped, as if struck by lightning as his lips and tongue touched her.

He worked on her until she was struggling not to scream from the pleasure he was giving. She grew wetter and wetter until the sheets beneath them were soaked with her nectar. His face was also soaked with her sweet honey.

"Good God, man!" she said, "Climb up here and fuck me."

As he moved her further up onto the bed and mounted her, Clint wondered if she'd had any sex since the death of her husband—whenever that was.

***

Julie thought long and hard about what Rosie Lee Reed wanted with Clint Adams. She hadn't known Clint very long, but she had come to feel protective of him. He had all but told her that he'd killed the two men who had gone after Rosie Lee. She was sure he would have offered her more help, more protection, but from what she knew about the girl, she would have turned him down. Everybody in town knew that the young madam was stubborn and independent. So the only reason she would be looking for Clint Adams now was that things had gotten worse, and she needed the assistance of the Gunsmith.

And Julie knew he would give it to her. After all, the first time he helped her, she hadn't even needed to ask.

In addition to Rosie Lee Reed, Julie was wondering what it was her mother was discussing with Clint. They didn't need any help with their hotel. Was there something else that was bothering her mother?

Julie knew she needed the answers to all these questions.

Chapter Fourteen

"Well," Helen said, "I guess you deserve some of your reputation."

Clint couldn't believe the woman just had sex with him, in an effort to keep him from being interested in Julie. There had to be another reason. Maybe she was hoping he would help her with some problem.

But she seemed very calm, as they lay naked together, side-by-side, on his bed.

"Helen, I have to go—"

"No, wait," she said, putting a hand out, keeping him from rising. "I need one more thing."

She rolled on top of him, kissed him urgently, then started moving down his body until her head was between his legs. She took his penis into her mouth and sucked it until it was rock hard. The first time he took her, he had been on top. Now, it seemed she wanted to be on top.

She climbed up, trapping his hard cock between them. She moved on him, rubbing his cock against her vagina, wetting him thoroughly, then lifting her hips and coming down on him, taking him deep inside.

"Oh God," she said, pressing her hands down on him and beginning to ride him up-and-down.

He was waiting for her to climax on him, squeezing him tightly as she fought for her release. But before that could happen, he felt his own release well up inside him and, as he erupted inside her, he almost lost consciousness . . .

***

She watched him as he got dressed, propping herself up on one elbow.

"Will this keep you away from my daughter?" she asked.

"You had nothing to worry about, Helen," Clint said. "You didn't have to do this to keep me away from Julie."

"I think I knew that," she said, rolling onto her back. "I think I did this mostly for my own benefit. I mean, it's been a while . . ."

Suddenly, there was a knock on the door. Helen seemed to panic. She leaped from the bed with the sheet wrapped around her.

"That might be Julie!" she hissed. "She can't know—"

"Stand off to one side," he told her, "out of sight of the door."

She did, flattening her back against the wall.

"Who is it?" he asked.

"It's Julie."

Helen closed her eyes and bit her lip.

"What can I do for you, Julie?" Clint asked.

"My mother said she was coming up here to talk to you," Julie said. "Have you seen her?"

"I did, but that was earlier."

"Um, can you open the door?"

"I was washing myself," he said. "I'm not exactly presentable, right now."

"Well, all right . . . I have a message for you."

"From who?"

"Rosie Lee Reed," Julie said. "She came to the hotel looking for you. Apparently, she wants to talk to you about something. I told her you weren't available, but she asked if you could go to her house."

"Oh," he said, "all right, then. I'll get dressed and do that."

"I'm going to see if I can find my mother," she said. "I'll see you downstairs."

"Fine, see you later."

As Julie walked away, they heard her footsteps fade. Helen heaved a huge sigh of relief.

"You better get dressed and figure out what you're going to tell your daughter."

"What are you going to do?" she asked, dropping the sheet and grabbing her clothes.

"I'll go and see what Miss Reed wants."

"She's a whore, what do you think she wants?"

"As I told Julie, she's a madam, not necessarily a whore. And she's a young girl, about Julie's age. She might need help."

"Her reputation is for bein' very independent. And I wouldn't exactly compare her to my daughter."

"Maybe not," Clint said, "but I'm going to see what she wants." He opened the door. "What are you going to tell Julie?"

"I'll think of something."

"Good luck."

"You, too."

He slipped out into the hall and closed the door behind him.

***

When Clint got to the lobby Julie was behind the desk.

"You find your mom?" he asked.

"No," she said. "I guess I'll just wait here for her to show up. Are you going to that whorehouse?"

"I'm going to see the Reed, girl."

"Sorry," Julie said, "I didn't mean—the place is called The Doll House."

"That's an interesting name."

"Be careful," Julie told him. "It's filled with young girls."

"I'll do the best I can," he said, and left the hotel.

Chapter Fifteen

As Clint approached the Doll House it looked very quiet. He went up the steps and tried the door, found it locked. He knocked and waited. The door was opened by a small, blonde girl.

"We're not open," she told him.

"I'm here to see Rosie Lee," Clint said. "She asked me to come."

"Are you Mr. Adams?" the girl asked.

"Yes, I am."

"I'm Goldie," the blonde said. "I'll take you to Rosie."

Clint entered and looked around at the carnage. It seemed like every stick of furniture in the place had been smashed.

"What the hell happened here?"

"Five men broke in and destroyed all our furniture," Goldie said.

"Did they put those bruises on your face, too?" Clint asked.

Goldie touched her face and said, "Yes, and on other girls, as well. They all but killed Charlie."

"Charlie?"

"Charlie Moon," Goldie said. "He looks after all the girls, but five men were too much for him. Follow me. Rosie is this way."

She led Clint down a hall to a closed door. She knocked, but opened it without waiting for a reply.

"Rosie, Mr. Adams is here," Goldie said.

"Let him come in."

Goldie stood aside to allow Clint to enter a small office. Rosie Lee was sitting behind a desk.

"You can go, Goldie," Rosie said.

"Yes, Ma'am."

Goldie closed the door behind her.

"Thank you for comin' Mr. Adams."

"Just call me Clint," he said. "I'm sorry I wasn't in the hotel when you came by."

"That's all right, you're here now. Please sit. This room is the only place on the first floor that still has furniture."

"Then I assume the men who did the damage didn't go to the second floor?"

"No, they didn't. They stayed down here, busted the place up, and terrorized my girls."

"And they injured somebody named Charlie Moon?"

"Charlie's an Indian who looks after my girls. He also cooks and does odd jobs. He's very big, but there were five men."

"So I was told by Goldie."

"Charlie can usually handle any situation, but there were too many of them, this time."

"Were they sent by whoever sent those other two?"

"I assume they were," she said, "but I'm afraid I don't know who that is, or why."

"Has anyone recently tried to buy your business?" Clint asked.

"What? No."

"Then that might be what happens next," Clint suggested.

"You think this is because someone wants my business?" she asked.

"It's a guess," he said.

Rosie thought for a moment, then said, "No, it's a very good guess, I think. When do you figure they'll make their offer?"

"Fairly soon, I think," Clint said. "Probably before you get some new furniture."

"They kicked the door in, as well," Rosie said. "I'll fix it."

"And reinforce it?"

"Yes," she said. "Hopefully they won't get in so easily next time. And there *will* be a next time. That's why I came lookin' for you. "Without Charlie Moon, I need help."

"I've got my own business to tend to," he said, "but I'll do what I can."

Chapter Sixteen

"Where's Charlie Moon now?" Clint asked.

"He's in Doc Hicks' surgery," Rosie said. "Doc says he might make it if his skull isn't fractured."

"That's the kind of thing that you just have to wait and see," Clint said.

"And without Charlie, it's just me and my girls," Rosie said. "We have guns, but most of them have never used one."

"Well, I can fix that," Clint said. "I'll give them some lessons."

"And then what?" she asked. "Leave us to take care of your own business? I can pay you—"

"I'm not going to leave until I know you and your girls are safe," he said, cutting her off. "And I don't need to be paid."

"So we have to wait and see who comes to me with an offer," Rosie said.

"That sounds like the way to go," Clint said. "Do you have a competitor in town?"

"There are other whores in town, but not all in one house," she said. "I don't see anyone considering us competition."

"What about a group in town, like a band of women wanting you closed down?"

"Enough to hire those men? I doubt it. Besides, I've never heard of any such group."

"So nobody's ever tried to close you down? The Town Council? The Mayor?"

"They're all customers of mine," she said, smiling.

"Then we're back to waiting for someone to come forward and try to buy you out."

"Good, when that happens you shoot 'em."

"There are some things we can try before resorting to that."

"I thought your guns were always your first resort," she said.

"That's because you don't know me."

"If you were a friend of my mom, that was always her first choice," Rosie said.

"You're talking about Belle's reputation, not her personality."

"You knew her twenty years ago," Rosie said. "She may have changed."

"Well, unless she's the one trying to close you down, I don't think we'll have to worry about her, do you?"

"No, we shouldn't," Rosie said. "Belle knows I don't really want anything to do with her."

"And why's that?"

"I have enough problems without everyone knowing I'm Belle Starr's daughter."

Clint figured that was probably true.

"I appreciate you taking the time to help, even while you're still searching."

"Well, I can't see walking away from you and your young ladies when you might still be in danger."

"I'd like you to walk me over to the doctor's surgery so I can check on Charlie Moon."

"Why don't I walk your girls through the lessons with a gun, and then we can do that. How many girls do you have?"

"Right now, half a dozen."

"So seven, including you."

"Right."

"How are you with that derringer of yours?"

"I can shoot," Rosie said, "but it's a good idea for you to work with the girls. We have enough guns in the house for all of them."

"Then let's get started on that," he suggested.

"I'll have Goldie gather the girls in the front sitting room.

"Good," Clint said, "and bring your derringer."

"I'm carryin' it with me at all times."

Chapter Seventeen

Clint addressed Rosie and her girls in the sitting room, going through the steps of properly firing a pistol. Several of the girls preferred rifles, so he worked some extra time with them while Rosie went back to her office.

When he was done, he joined her and asked, "Ready?"

"How are the girls?"

"Scared," Clint said, "but they should be able to defend themselves."

"Then let's go and check on Charlie," she said.

They walked out of the house and headed for the doctor's office.

***

"Miss Reed," Doc Hicks said, when they entered his office.

"How's Charlie, Doc?"

"Still unconscious, otherwise he seems fine."

"Will he wake up?" Clint asked.

Hicks frowned at Clint.

"Doc, this is Clint Adams."

"The Gunsmith?"

"He's agreed to help me until Charlie's back on his feet," she said. "When will that be?"

"I don't think his skull was fractured, but it may still be some time before he wakes up."

"Can we see him?" Rosie asked.

"Of course. He's in there." Hicks indicated a closed door.

"Thank you," she said, and led Clint into the next room.

Charlie Moon was lying on his back in a large bed. He looked like he was sleeping.

"Wow," Clint said, "he's a big man. I can see how it took five men to bring him down."

Rosie approached the bed and put her hand on the Indian's head.

"Poor Charlie," she said, stroking his brow.

"How long have you known him?" Clint asked.

"Since I was a kid," she said. "He's almost like a father to me." She looked at Clint. "I want to know who did this to him."

"The girls saw the five men who attacked your house," he pointed out.

"No," Rosie said, "I want to know who sent them. That's the one I want."

"Well," Clint said, "then we'll try to find out. Meanwhile, he'll be safe here."

"Let's talk to the doc about that," she said.

***

"I'll have a man stand watch over him," Doc Hicks said. "I doubt anyone will break in here, but I'll see that he's safeguarded."

"Thank you, Doc."

"Doc, I'm at the Alabaman, in case you need me," Clint said.

"Helen Dexter's hotel," he said. "Does she know who you are?"

"She knows."

"I hope her hotel doesn't receive the same treatment your place did," Hicks said to Rosie.

"I don't see why it would," she said. "Whoever's behind this did it to hurt me. I don't have any connection to the Dexters'."

"I hope you're right."

"Doc, let me know right away if there's any change in his condition."

"I will."

"Thank you."

Rosie and Clint left the doctor's surgery and stopped out front.

"Do you think we should move him?" she asked.

"To where? If they want him, they'll get him. But whoever tried to hurt you may not want to harm the town doctor."

"That's true."

"Let's get back to your house," Clint said. "I'd like to find out if any of your girls have seen the man I'm looking for."

***

Once again, Clint gathered the girls in the sitting room. He could hear the hammering from the carpenter making some repairs.

He gave the girls a description of Del Thaxton, and asked if any of them had been with him, or seen him.

"That sounds like one ugly man," Goldie said. "I haven't seen him."

The other girls also shook their heads. Since Rosie wasn't reopening the place yet, Clint dismissed the girls to their rooms, and went to Rosie's office.

"Any luck?" she asked, looking up at him as he entered.

"No," Clint said, "Thaxton has apparently never been in your place."

"I'm sorry they were no help to you," she said. "And I'm sorry I'm keeping you from your hunt."

"It's all right," Clint said. "I'll find him, eventually."

"He must've killed a good friend of yours."

"We weren't as close as you and Charlie Moon were, but we were friends. And there was no reason to kill him. He was simply on the street when Thaxton and his men came out of the bank, and Thaxton shot him."

"And his men?"

"The law caught them, but Thaxton got away."

"Why are you hunting him, and not letting the posse?" Rosie asked him.

"They followed until he left their jurisdiction. They're adhering to the law by not continuing." He sat down in the chair in front of her desk. "I, on the other hand, don't have to stick to any rules."

Chapter Eighteen

"You want a drink?" she asked. "I have some whiskey. Or maybe you prefer wine?"

"I'm not much of a whiskey drinker, but I could go for a glass about now."

She rose from behind her desk and walked to a sideboard. She poured Clint a whiskey and brought it to him.

"None for you?"

"I don't drink," she said, reseating herself.

"What's all this?" he asked, indicating the paperwork on her desk.

"I'm figuring out how much the repairs are going to cost me."

Clint sipped his whiskey and put it down on her desk. The sip was enough to remind him that he really didn't like it.

"Do you have the funds?" he asked.

"I have some," she said. "Luckily they only did damage to the front of the house."

"And the girls?"

"I'm going to have them go to the doctor's office two at a time, and armed."

"We can give each of them a derringer," Clint said.

"I can do that," she said. She eyed the whiskey Clint had left in his glass, then picked it up and tossed it down. She shivered and sat back in her chair. "I don't see why people like that stuff."

"Frankly, neither do I."

"Rosie, can you come up with any suggestions for someone who might want to buy you out or shut you down?"

"None," she said. "I don't associate with many people in town outside of this place."

"Which means you only associate with men."

She nodded and said, "Men who want a poke."

"That means there could be any number of wives in town who'd like to shut you down."

"My clientele is mostly regulars, married men who either don't get it at home, or don't want to get it at home."

"Can you give me a list of names?"

"Sure. Are you going to talk to their wives?" she asked, while writing the list.

"It's all I can think to do while we wait," he admitted.

"Well, here you go." She held the list out to him. It had names and addresses where he could find them.

"Eight?"

"It used to be more, but some of them moved away, and some stopped coming."

He handed her back the list.

"Add the names of the men who stopped coming. We might as well include everyone who's still in town."

"All right." She wrote three more names.

There was a knock on the door as she handed the list back to him.

"Come in!"

The door opened and Goldie stuck her head in.

"What is it?" she asked.

"Henry Moon's here."

"Let him in."

As Goldie withdrew, Clint asked, "*Henry* Moon?"

"Charlie's cousin. He probably wants to know what happened."

"Do you think he'd want to help find out who did this to Charlie?"

"I don't know," she said. "They're very different."

"In what way?"

"You'll see."

When the door opened and a man stepped in, Clint saw what she meant. Henry Moon looked like a half-sized Indian.

Chapter Nineteen

"Hello, Henry," Rosie said, rising to greet the man.

"Miss Reed," the man said, executing a slight bow to her. She gave him a brief hug.

"This is Clint Adams. He's agreed to help me."

Henry Moon turned to face Clint. No expression on his face, which seemed to be made of stone. Clint would later see the resemblance between the two cousins, but while Charlie Moon looked to be six-and-a-half feet tall, Henry was a foot shorter. The man's short sleeved shirt, though, made it clear they had roughly the same sized biceps.

"I am here, Miss Reed, to hear what happened to my cousin, Charlie."

"Well," she said, "have a seat, Henry, and I'll tell you."

When he sat she asked, "Whiskey?"

"Yes."

She poured a glass and brought it to him.

"Thank you," he said, then tossed the drink back and set the empty glass down on the desk.

"Another?" she asked.

"No. Tell me what happened."

Clint sat silently listening as Rosie explained to Henry what had happened to his cousin.

"Where is Charlie?" Henry asked, when Rosie finished.

"He's still at the doctor's," she said. "Doc Hicks wants to keep him there until he wakes up."

"His skull was not fractured?" Henry asked.

"The doc doesn't think so," Clint said," but he won't know until your cousin wakes up."

"Do you know who sent those men here?" Henry asked.

"No," she said. "Clint is going to try to find out who it was."

"If he is here protecting you, how will he do that?" Henry asked.

"I was just talking with Rosie about that. I was going to ask if she knew of anyone who could help."

"What kind of help?" the Indian asked.

"We would need someone to stay here, well-armed, to protect the girls."

"Clint believes someone will come to try to buy me out," Rosie said. "We don't know what will happen when I say no."

"I will stay here and protect your property and your girls," Henry said to Rosie. "That will allow Mr. Adams to ask his questions."

"Rosie has some weapons here," Clint said. "I've worked a bit with the girls so they know how to shoot. You can choose whatever weapon—"

"I have my own," Henry said. "A shotgun. It is on my horse, outside."

"Good," Clint said. "I'll walk out with you, so you can get it."

Henry stood and looked at Rosie. "I will be back."

He and Clint left Rosie's office together and walked out to Henry Moon's pinto. The Indian removed his double-barrel shotgun from his horse and turned to face Clint.

"You wanted to walk out with me and say something without Rosie hearing it."

"How long have you known her?" Clint asked.

"What you mean is, how long has she known me," Henry restated. "Charlie and I have known her since she was very small."

"So you know who her mother is?"

"Yes," Henry said. "Belle Starr."

"I knew Belle Starr years ago," Clint said. "Rosie has her mother's stubbornness. If someone does show up here with an offer to buy her out, make sure she doesn't go overboard."

"I will stand by her every moment," Henry promised. "But if someone tries to harm her, I will have to kill them. It is my belief that Charlie was taken down because he was trying not to kill anyone." Henry set his jaw firm before adding, "I will not make that same mistake."

Chapter Twenty

When Clint left the Doll House, he felt sure that Henry Moon would do what had to be done to protect Rosie Lee Reed and avenge his cousin.

Clint had a long list of people to question. It wouldn't be a long process though. He felt fairly sure he would be able to judge whether or not these men had wives who would take SUCH a drastic tactic to keep their husbands away from The Doll House.

At the same time, he had to be on the lookout for Del Thaxton. He couldn't forget his main reason for being in Clanton, Alabama.

But it was late afternoon when he left Rosie Reed's house. She had written on her list where he could find the men during the day, when they were working. He didn't know where these men lived with their wives. And, in truth, he wanted to question the women more than the men. He wanted to watch their reaction when he asked about the Doll House.

Two of the men were bartenders and would probably be tending bar all night. He decided to go to the two saloons first.

One was called the Split Branch Saloon, and the other simply The No. 5. Clint decided he would go to the Split Branch first, but on the way he found himself across the street from the sheriff's office, so he stopped in.

Sheriff Poole looked surprised when Clint walked in. He was just getting to his feet.

"I was gettin' ready to go and get somethin' to eat," the man said.

"This won't take long."

The lawman sat down behind his desk.

"What's on your mind?"

"You know what happened to Rosie Reed at the General Store," Clint said.

"I do, indeed."

"Has anyone told you what happened at her house?" Clint asked.

"Somethin' happened after she got back?"

Clint shook his head.

"No," he said, "while she was on her way to the store, five men broke into her place, smashed furniture, abused the girls, and almost killed Charlie Moon."

"Charlie? I wouldn't think even five men could do that."

"They hit him over the head several times," Clint said. "The doctor is still trying to determine whether or not they cracked his skull."

"Jesus!" Poole said. "Poor Charlie. Does Henry know?"

"He does," Clint said. "He's at Rosie's right now, keeping watch."

"You think they'll come back?"

"I think whoever sent them will try to buy Rosie out," Clint said. "Henry's there to look after her."

"Does he have his shotgun with him?"

"He does."

Poole shook his head.

"Henry's a lot meaner than Charlie," he said. "He'll blow off some heads before he takes a beatin'—especially from white men."

"They're quite a mismatched pair of cousins," Clint said.

"You got that right," Poole said. "From appearances you'd think Charlie was the mean one, but believe me, it's Henry."

"I don't care how mean he is, as long as he keeps Rosie safe."

"Why are you gettin' involved in this?" Poole asked.

"I don't like what they tried to do to Rosie at the General Store. But I was done after that, until Rosie came to my hotel to ask for help. Frankly, I don't understand why she didn't come to you."

"Rosie Reed don't have much use for lawmen. I think she made the right decision."

"Does that mean you have some idea who's behind the attack?" Clint asked.

"Not hardly," Sheriff Poole said.

"Are you taking any steps to try to find out?" Clint asked.

"Like I said, Rosie's got no use for the law, so I guess finding out who was behind it is gonna be up to you."

"I'm thinking about the wives in town, who aren't happy about their husbands patronizing The Doll House."

"You really think a woman could've been behind the attack?" Poole asked.

"Or women," Clint said. "Maybe more than one. Hiring those men was probably an expensive proposition. Some of the wives could've joined forces."

"How would a bunch of women know who to hire?" Poole asked.

"It's not a huge town, Sheriff," Clint said. "Troublemakers have a way of standing out."

"That's true enough."

"In fact," Clint went on, "I'd think you'd have some idea who these men were, and who hired them."

"Well," Poole said, "if I was you, I'd start lookin' in a couple of the lower rent saloons."

"That was my plan," Clint said.

"Then I wish you luck," Poole said, "but if you go into those places alone, you really will be lookin' for trouble."

"I don't usually have to look for trouble," Clint said. "It usually just finds me."

Chapter Twenty-One

Clint walked to the Split Branch Saloon, wondering if he was making a mistake. Would anyone's wife really pay to have The Doll House busted up, the girls bruised, and Charlie Moon almost killed?

The Split Branch looked exactly like what Sheriff Poole called a low rent saloon. The sign with the name over the door was hanging down on one side, one of the batwings doors was crooked, and the inside looked as if it hadn't seen the right end of a broom or mop in weeks.

It was dusk, a time when saloons started to fill up, but this one wasn't even half full. A bored looking bartender was moving dirt around on the bar, with a dirty rag. He looked like he was in his early fifties, with grey/black stubble on his face. There was a look of intense sadness on his face.

"Are you Gil Martin?" Clint asked.

"Who wants to know?" He continued moving the rag around on the bar.

"My name's Clint Adams."

The rag stopped.

"I'm Martin," the bartender said. "You the Gunsmith?"

"That's right."

"What the hell are ya doin' here?" Martin asked.

"I want to talk to you."

"Me? About what? Who sent ya?"

"I was given your name by Rosie Lee Reed."

A panicked look came over Martin's face.

"Not so loud!" he hissed. "Why'd she send you here?"

"She told me you're a customer."

"I used to be," Martin said. "Not anymore, not since my wife found out."

"Actually, I wanted to talk to you about your wife."

"Agnes?" Martin said. "What about her?"

"Did you hear what happened at the Doll House this morning?"

Martin leaned his elbows on the bar.

"What happened?"

"Five men broke in, ransacked the place, abused the girls and almost killed Charlie Moon."

"Charlie?" Martin said. "Who did all that?"

"We don't know," Clint said. "Two men also attacked Rosie as she was coming out of the general store. They said they were sent."

"By who? Hey, wait, you don't think—"

"I'm trying to find out," Clint said.

"Why don't you ask them who sent them?"

"When I find the man, I will," Clint said. "Two of them are dead."

"Who killed—oh." Martin straightened up and backed away from Clint. "Why are ya askin' me?"

"I was wondering what kind of woman your wife was?" Clint asked. "Would she hire something like that done to keep you away from there?"

"Are you crazy?" Martin asked. "You see where I work. We ain't got the money for that."

"Do you know other men whose wives might do it?" Clint asked. "Maybe they joined forces and put the money together?"

"Wives?" Martin laughed. "I can see my wife killin' me if she caught me there again. But I don't see her— look, my wife's an unpleasant woman. She's got no friends."

"What about some friends of yours?"

"You're lookin' at this all wrong, friend," Martin said. "Sure, me and a bunch of my friends used to go to Rosie's, and then our wives found out. They got mad and threatened to leave us, but there's no way any of them would put up money to hurt Rosie and the girls."

"Are you sure?"

"I'm—well, yeah, I'm sure." But Martin didn't look very sure.

Chapter Twenty-Two

As he left the Split Branch Clint felt foolish for thinking that a woman or women might be responsible for the attacks on Rosie Lee and The Doll House. Rather than wasting time talking to men who were afraid of their wives, he was probably better off remaining at the house, awaiting an offer to buy. Also, in the event of a second attack, his presence would be necessary. Between him and Henry Moon, they should be able to fight off such an eventuality.

When Clint got back to The Doll House, he was surprised to see the building all lit up. He had to knock on the door to get in. Goldie opened it and stepped back to allow him to enter. Clint heard voices and laughter from the sitting room.

"What's going on?" he asked, as she closed the door.

"We're open for business," she told him.

"I didn't know Rosie was going to reopen."

"She just decided about an hour ago."

"And you have customers, already?"

"Word got out fast," Goldie said.

"Where's Rosie?" he asked.

"In her office."

"And Henry?"

"He's standing watch in the sitting room."

"And you?"

"I'm on the door."

"You don't go upstairs with a man?"

"I'm not experienced enough, yet."

"Okay," he said. "I'm going to see Rosie. I know the way."

He started away, then turned back.

"The customers in the sitting room," he said, "are they regulars?"

"Yes."

"How many?"

"There are five."

"Has anyone gone upstairs, yet?"

"No," Goldie said. "They're having drinks and making their choices."

"Don't let anyone go upstairs until you hear from me," he told her.

"Yessir."

Clint walked down the hall to the door of Rosie's office and knocked.

"Come in!" she shouted.

He opened the door and entered.

"You're back already?"

"I changed my mind about what I'm going to do," he said. "I can't imagine somebody's irate wife was behind the attacks,"

"You can't imagine how furious some of these wives can get," Rosie told him.

"Have any of them ever come here?"

"No."

"All right, let's put wives aside for now," he said, sitting across from her. "Why did you decide to open for business tonight?"

"I'm not going to let anyone put me out of business," she said, "and that's what not opening tonight would mean."

"Rosie—"

"My mind's made up, Clint," she said, firmly. "I'm not closing down."

"I understand," Clint said.

Rosie sat back in her chair and stared at him.

"You're not going to try to convince me to close?"

"Not even temporarily. If someone is going to make you an offer, I think they should see that you're very much still in business."

"And if they just come chargin' in, again?" she asked.

"They won't find it so easy, this time. Henry and I will be ready for them."

"And if nothing happens?"

"I don't think that's an option," he said. "They've already made two tries. I expect them to get more active, not less."

Chapter Twenty-Three

Clint left Rosie's office and made his way to the front of the house. Goldie had just let another customer in and was showing him to the sitting room. As he entered, he saw the girls sharing sofas and divans, sitting next to and on a bunch of happy looking men. In one corner, standing with his arms folded, was Henry Moon. He managed to acknowledge Clint's present without moving a muscle. Clint nodded to him, put his back to the wall and looked around.

Rosie had not been kidding about the ages of her girls. Some of them looked to Clint like teenagers in garish makeup stolen from their mothers. Their dresses revealed lots of bosom and thigh, even though some of the girls were too skinny for it. But two or three of the girls had enough weight on them to make the dresses sexy.

There was a man in one chair, a blonde girl on his lap, with his laughing face buried on her impressive bosom. Another man seemed very satisfied with a flat-chested brunette, whose dark-nipples were on display. From what Clint could see, Henry Moon was watching the men, and ignoring the girls.

Eventually, a couple of the girls grabbed some man's hands, led them from the room, and up the stairs. Clint looked at Henry, who seemed to get the message. The Indian followed them up the stairs and took up his position in the hall, arms folded. He would move at the first sign or sound of trouble from a room.

Clint took up a position at the open doorway of the sitting room, so he could see the entire interior, as well as the hallway and the stairs.

As time passed, some of the girls came down with their customers and saw them off, others took men upstairs. From the bottom of the stairs, Clint could see Henry Moon standing at the top.

In time Rosie came from her office. She conversed briefly with Goldie to get an idea of how business was going and then walked over to join Clint.

"Goldie says we've had mostly regulars, tonight."

"What about non-regulars?" he asked.

"A few, but she's sure they're all townspeople."

"So no strangers."

"Apparently, not."

"I'm thinking if someone comes to make you an offer, it'll be in the morning, not during business hours. If I was wrong, I'd expect to see more strangers here."

"That way if I say no, they'll attack again, from inside."

"Right."

"And we wouldn't have to worry about that if I hadn't reopened."

"Right again."

"All right," she said, "if we get through this night with no trouble, I'll run my intentions by you."

"No argument from me."

"I'm going to have one of the girls cook something," Rosie said. "I don't know how good it will be. Charlie does all the cooking."

"As long as it's something," he said. "Do you normally feed your customers?"

"No," Rosie said, "the food is just for us."

"What time do you close?"

"I try to have the men out by two a.m.," she said. "Then we all eat, and the girls turn in."

"And you?"

"I'm usually in my office til five. Then I turn in and try to sleep til noon."

"Is there a bed I can use?"

"Plenty of them," she said. "I'll have one outfitted with clean sheets."

"Thanks," he said. "I appreciate the consideration."

She looked at the small watch on her wrist.

"I'll have Goldie stop letting customers in. Then I'll have her cook."

"Is she any good?"

Rosie smiled.

"I'll just say she's a better cook than she is a whore."

Chapter Twenty-Four

When Clint woke the next morning it was only eight a.m. Rosie wouldn't be up for four more hours. Clint had turned in at three-thirty with Rosie still in her office. But there was no way he could sleep past eight.

He dressed and went downstairs to the kitchen. Several of the girls were already eating breakfast, while Goldie was at the stove.

"Breakfast, Mr. Adams?" she said.

"Please and call me Clint."

She smiled and asked, "Flapjacks and sausages?"

"Perfect."

He sat. The girl next to him looked at him and said, "We usually have eggs, but we're out."

Goldie put a plate in front of Clint and said to the girl, "You and me, we'll go get some from the General Store."

"What?" the girl said "Well, yeah, okay, if Rosie says it's okay."

"She will," Goldie said.

"B-but those men—"

"Ella," Goldie said, "she'll send Henry Moon with us. We'll be fine."

Ella looked at Clint.

"What do you think?"

"I think if we need eggs we'll have to go and get some." He swallowed and said to Goldie, "This is real good."

"Do me a favor, tell Rosie," Goldie said. "Maybe she'll give me the job permanent-like."

"You really don't wanna be a whore, do ya?" a girl on the other side of the table asked.

"I'm just not good at it," Goldie said. "But I can cook."

"You sure can," Clint said.

"More, Clint?"

"Please."

She fixed Clint another plate, then a plate each for two more girls who came in. Clint only had a couple of names fixed, so far.

The next to enter the kitchen was Henry Moon. Clint couldn't tell by looking at the Indian if he had slept or not, but he knew Rosie had let Henry use Charlie's room.

"Breakfast, Henry?" Goldie asked.

The Indian nodded and sat.

"Flapjacks and sausage?" she asked.

"No sausage," Henry said.

"Comin' up," Goldie said.

Henry sat across from Clint, who looked at him and asked, "Get any sleep?"

"No," Henry said.

"Aren't you tired?"

"I do not need much sleep." Goldie put a plate in front of him. "But I do need food," he continued, and started eating.

One-by-one the girls finished eating and left the kitchen, until only Clint and Henry were left. At eleven a.m. Rosie came in, wearing a robe like the other girls.

"You're up early," Goldie said.

"I didn't sleep very well," Rosie said, taking a seat. Goldie came over and put a plate in front of her.

"No eggs?" She complained.

"We're out," Goldie said. "Me and Ella can go get some today."

"I don't want anyone going out," Rosie said.

"You can send Henry with us," Goldie said.

"They should be okay," Clint said.

"Yeah, okay," Rosie said, after a few moments, "eggs and some other stuff. I'll give you a list. Get dressed."

"I'll tell Ella." Goldie started out of the kitchen but stopped. "I'll clean up in here when I get back. There's a few more flapjacks on the stove."

"Good,"

As Goldie left the kitchen Rosie asked Clint, "You really think I should let her go?"

"I think the less people there are in the building, the more likely somebody will come with an offer. You might even want to send a few more girls, with her."

Rosie shrugged and said, "Why not? Just let me finish my breakfast and I'll gather them up. I'm sure they'll all like to go shopping."

Clint stood to leave the kitchen and said, "But don't let them forget the eggs."

***

Clint was sitting in the front room when the girls came down, dressed for shopping. He didn't realize they were all going to go, but that was just as well. Henry Moon came down behind them.

"Do you wanna come, Clint?" Goldie asked.

"No, thanks," he said. "You all have a good time."

"We will."

"And—"

"I know," she said, "don't forget the eggs."

"No," Clint said, "I was going to ask if any of you had guns."

"We have Henry," Goldie said, "but a couple of us have derringers."

"Then stay together," Clint said, "Just in case."

Chapter Twenty-Five

After all the girls and Henry had left, Rosie came down from her room, dressed for the day in jeans and a man's work shirt. By the time they opened for business later in the day, she would be wearing a revealing gown.

For now, she entered the sitting room and sat across from Clint.

"Do you expect someone to come by today?" she asked.

"Considering there have already been two attacks on you, I don't think whoever's behind it will waste too much time," Clint said.

"I'd like to get it over with so we know who we're dealing with."

"We may not find that out, right away," Clint said. "I suspect whoever's actually behind it all will send someone to represent them. When someone does come, I'll likely have to follow them."

"Why does this have to be so complicated?" Rosie whined. "Why can't they just walk in, make their offer, be turned down and go away?"

"Nothing is ever that easy."

"My life's been difficult up til now, so why should I expect it to change?" she asked.

"Well, you haven't exactly picked the easiest way to make a living," Clint said.

"If I'm left alone to ply my trade, I can do very well," she told him. "All I need is to be left alone."

"We'll see what we can do about that."

At that point there was a knock at the door.

"Okay," he said, "either they were watching and saw everybody else leave, or someone's just trying to find out if you're open."

Suddenly, her derringer was in her hand. Clint hadn't seen where it came from.

"There's only one way to find out," she said.

"I'll stand behind the door," he said and they moved.

When she unlocked the door and opened it, she kept her right hand with the derringer down at her side. Clint was behind the door.

A well-dressed man in his forties looked at her in surprise.

"Miss Reed?"

"That's right," she said. "We're not open right now. Come back in a few hours."

"I'm sorry," he said, "I'm not here as a customer for your lovely girls."

"Then why are you here?"

"I have a business proposition for you. May I come in so we may discuss it?"

"Why not."

She stepped back to allow him to enter. That was when he saw the derringer in her hand, and Clint stepping out from behind the door.

"I'm sorry," he said. "Am I interrupting something?"

"Not at all," Rosie said. "Follow me to my office."

"Lead the way."

She did, and Clint took up the rear. The man looked back at him a couple of times.

"Have a seat," Rosie said, sitting at her desk. "Can I get you something? Coffee? Whiskey?"

"Uh, no thank you." The man sat, but still seemed concerned about having Clint behind him. "Uh, will this gentleman be staying during our conversation?" he asked.

"I'm sorry," she said. "This is Mr. Adams. And yes, he will be staying."

The man seemed to be waiting for more of an explanation, but eventually he turned fully to face Rosie and said, "All right, then."

"What's your name?" Rosie asked.

"I am Louis Medford," the man said, digging into his vest pocket. "My card."

He passed it over to Rosie, who then held it out to Clint. It read:

LOUIS MEDFORD, ATTORNEY-AT-LAW

"You're a lawyer," Clint said.

"That's correct."

"So does that mean you're here representing a client?" Clint asked.

"Right again."

"And who would that be?" Rosie asked.

Medford turned to face her again, and Clint remained behind him to keep the man off balance.

"I'm not at liberty to say, at the moment," Medford said.

"Then why are you here?" Clint asked.

Medford turned so that he was half facing Clint and Rosie.

"My client would like to buy your establishment."

"I don't want to sell," Rosie said.

"But you haven't heard the offer," the lawyer said.

"I don't have to," Rosie said. "I'm not interested."

Medford frowned.

"I'm afraid my client won't be happy to hear that."

"Then he'll just have to be unhappy," Rosie said.

Chapter Twenty-Six

"Mr. Medford," Clint said, stepping forward so the man could now see them both, "there have been two attacks, one on this building, and one on Miss Reed. Was your client behind that?"

"What? No! No, he would never do anything like that," Medford insisted.

"Are you sure?" Clint asked. "How long has he been your client?"

"Well . . . not very long," Medford said. "In fact, this is the first job I've done for him."

"Making this offer?" Rosie asked.

"Yes, and if you would allow me to give you his offer—" Medford said.

"I don't want to hear it," Rosie said. "I'm not interested."

"But—"

Clint put his hand on the lawyer's shoulder.

"You heard the lady," he said. "She's not interested. Now tell me who your client is."

"I can't do that," Medford said. "It's privileged information."

"All right, then bring him a message from us," Clint said. "Rosie's not selling, and if he sends his men after her again, he'll have to deal with me. And I'll find out who he is, and I'll come after him. Got it?"

"I understand what you're saying," the lawyer said, "but I don't understand why. I can't believe my client would ever do something like that."

"Why does he want to buy this business?" Clint asked. "Why's he want a whorehouse?"

"I—I didn't ask him that," Medford said. "I'm just here to present his offer."

"Well, go back and tell him it never got offered," Rosie said. "I don't want to hear it."

Medford took a deep breath and stood up.

"Very well," he said. "I'll bring him your reply."

"Mr. Adams will see you out," Rosie said.

"I'll be right behind you," Clint said to Medford, who nodded and went into the hall.

Clint leaned over and said to Rosie, "I'm going to follow him. Lock the door after I leave."

"Right."

Clint went out into the hall and walked the waiting lawyer to the front door.

"I don't suppose you would be able to talk any sense into the young lady."

"This young lady knows exactly what she wants," Clint said.

The two men walked outside and down the steps, where they stopped.

"Thank you for your time," Medford said.

"You're welcome."

The lawyer started to walk away, then stopped and turned back.

"Mr. Adams," he called, "in case your intention is to follow me, I have an office on Kentucky Street."

"Kentucky Street?"

"The rent is not as bad as Front Street or Maple."

Clint watched the man walk away. There was no point in following him if he really had an office on Kentucky Street, but of course he could have been lying. Or he might be going to see his client, rather then to his own office.

He decided to go ahead and follow him, anyway.

***

Clint followed Medford at a safe distance, which may not have been necessary. The man never stopped to look behind him once. Eventually, he turned on Kentucky Street. Clint remained on the corner and watched. When the man went inside about halfway down the street, Clint walked to the building. There was a shingle hanging there that said:

LOUIS MEDFORD, ATTORNEY-AT-LAW

Satisfied that the man really had an office there, Clint started walking back. He considered waiting across the street, in case the man left to go and see his client, but he doubted Medford would do that so soon—especially since he knew Clint had followed him. He was going to have to figure out another way. Meanwhile, he wasn't comfortable leaving Rosie alone, so he rushed back.

***

When Rosie opened the door for him, she asked. "Where'd he go?"

"He went to his office, on Kentucky Street."

They walked back to her office.

"That's not a high rent area," she said, seating herself.

"Whoever his client is might have been more comfortable using a low rent lawyer to make his offer."

"So what will he do now?" she asked.

"He might send the offer, with a more reputable lawyer."

"Or?"

"He might decide to come at you again, this time with both barrels."

107

Chapter Twenty-Seven

When the girls returned to the house with Henry Moon, Goldie reported to Rosie.

"I got the eggs," she said, "but I'm surprised we got them home unbroken."

"Was there another attack?" Rosie asked.

"No, nothin' like that," Goldie said. "The girls had a fight, but I was able to stay out of it and protect the eggs."

"Who was fighting?" Rosie asked.

"Ella and Sherry wanted the same dress and fought over it. Delilah sided with Ella and Candy was on Sherry's side."

"What did Henry do?"

"He watched," Goldie said. "He didn't want to get involved any more than I did."

"I'll talk to all the girls involved," Rosie said. "Get the eggs into the kitchen."

Clint moved aside to allow Goldie to leave the office. He had stood against one wall to listen to Goldie's report.

"Do the girls often fight?" he asked Rosie.

"It's usually Ella and Sherry."

"It sounds like the responsible one is usually Goldie. And she can cook."

"I know," Rosie said. "The other girls are getting impatient, wanting me to put Goldie in a room, but the girl simply isn't ready to be a whore. She's too inexperienced. I wish I had a man who could break her in."

"If I was you, I'd simply make her a cook."

"We'll have to see how Charlie is when he comes back," Rosie said. "I guess I could make her his assistant for a while."

"Do we know how Charlie is?"

"I haven't talked to the doctor today," she said. "Maybe I should send Henry over there. I'm sure he'd like to know how his cousin is."

"I could pass the word along."

"Why don't you do that?" she asked. "I want you and me to be here in case something happens."

Clint nodded and said, "I'll tell him."

He left the office and found Henry in the front room. The girls were apparently all upstairs in their rooms with their new purchases.

"I heard there was some ruckus," Clint said.

"These women are crazy," Henry said.

"It's probably because they're so young," Clint said. "Listen, Rosie's wondering how Charlie's doing. She thought you might want to go to the doc's and find out."

"I would," Henry said. "Anything happen while we were gone?"

"A man came by and made an offer," Clint said.

"What man? What kind of offer?"

"Well, actually, he was a lawyer, but he wouldn't tell us who he was representing. He tried to make an offer, but Rosie wouldn't listen to it."

"How did he take it?"

"He said he'd go back to his client and tell him what she said."

"Tell *him*?"

"Yes," Clint said, "that takes care of my stupid theory about women joining forces."

"I didn't know about that."

"I was wondering if some irate wives had pooled their finances and hired the men who attacked."

"That sounds silly," Henry said.

"I agree," Clint said. "Even moreso now that we know it was a man behind the offer."

"But we still don't know if the man making this offer is the same one behind the attacks."

"That's true," Clint said. "Henry, you live here. If you find out from the sheriff the names of the two men I killed, maybe you'll be able to figure out who injured your cousin."

"I might," Henry said. "I'll go to the doctor's office, and then stop in on Sheriff Poole on the way back.

"And do you know a lawyer named Louis Medford? He has an office on Kentucky Street."

"I do not know him," Henry said. "If his office is on Kentucky Street, he cannot have many clients."

"Well," Clint said, "he's got at least one. And he didn't sound very stupid when he was talking to Rosie. He knew I was going to follow him, so he made sure to tell me where his office was."

"If he thought you were going to follow him, it does not sound very likely he will go to see his client today," Henry said. "Maybe I should visit the office in the morning and see where he goes."

"He'll be looking for a tail," Clint said.

"If I do not want him to see me," Henry said, "he won't see me. I do not attract attention like Charlie does."

"That makes sense," Clint said. "Okay, let's do that. But maybe you'll find out something from the sheriff. Or maybe you'll get something from Charlie if he wakes up."

"*When* he wakes up," Henry corrected. "My cousin has a hard head."

Chapter Twenty-Eight

When Henry Moon entered Doc Hicks' office the sawbones said, "He's stirring, but not conscious, yet."

"Is he going to die?"

"I don't think so."

"Will he wake?"

"Eventually," Hicks said.

"And when he wakes, will he be all right?"

"I think so."

"But we don't know when he will wake," Henry said.

"No, we don't."

"I want to know when he does," Henry said. "I want to know what he remembers from the attack. He might tell us who ordered it."

"I'll keep you informed," Hicks said.

"Good."

Henry went from the doctor's office to the sheriffs.

"Henry," Poole said, as he entered. "What brings you here? You hate the law."

"You know almost as many people from town as I do," Henry said. "Who were the two that Clint Adams killed?"

"Windham and Hanley."

Henry frowned.

"They would do anything for money," he said.

"They could've been hired by anyone," Poole said. "It's too bad Adams didn't take one alive."

"There are still at least five others," Henry pointed out.

"Well, Windham and Hanley usually worked alone," Poole said. "Knowing about them doesn't help identify the others."

"What about a lawyer named Medford?"

"On Kentucky Street?" Poole asked. "He's nobody, really. I don't know if he even has any clients."

"According to Clint, he has one."

"Have you met him?"

Henry shook his head.

"He came to the house to make an offer, but Rosie would not hear it."

"So you don't even know if this offer is connected to the attacks."

"No, we do not."

"Too bad. How's Charlie doin'?"

"My cousin is alive," Henry said. "The doctor thinks he will awake."

"When?"

"That the doctor does not know."

"Too bad," Poole said. "If he recognized any of the men who attacked him, that would be helpful."

"Indeed."

"Well, I'm sorry I can't help you, Henry."

"I am not surprised," Henry said, and left.

***

When Henry returned to the house, he found Clint in the sitting room and told him of his conversations with the doctor, and the lawman.

"So, nothing very helpful," Clint summed up.

"No," Henry said, "but my cousin will wake, eventually. We might have to wait until then."

I may not have that much time," Clint said. "I still have my own business to attend to."

"You're hunting a man," Henry said.

"Yes."

"What is his name?"

"Del Thaxton."

Henry shook his head.

"I do not know him."

Clint described Thaxton to the Indian, who shook his head, again.

"I have not seen such a man. Is he for hire?"

"Usually. What are you thinking?"

Henry shrugged.

"Maybe he was one of the five who injured Charlie. Is there any reason he would not work with others?"

"Not if there's enough money involved," Clint said.

"Why did you not think of that before now?"

"Because it would be a helluva coincidence."

"You do not like coincidence?"

"I hate it," Clint said, "but more than once I've had to deal with them."

"Perhaps this is such a time," Henry suggested.

"Maybe," Clint said, "guess we'll have to find that out."

Henry lifted his head and sniffed the air.

"Someone is cooking?" he asked.

"Goldie's making dinner for everyone," Clint said. "Perhaps we should go to the kitchen."

"I *am* hungry," Henry said.

"So am I."

They left the sitting room and walked down the hall to the kitchen. Several of the girls were already seated with steaming bowls in front of them.

"I bought the fixin's for beef stew," Goldie told them. "Have a seat."

She didn't have to tell them twice.

Chapter Twenty-Nine

While they were eating Rosie came in and joined them.

"I couldn't resist the smell," she said. Goldie put a bowl in front of her and she tasted it. "Is this Charlie's recipe?"

"No," Goldie said, over her shoulder, "it's mine."

"It's delicious, Goldie," Rosie said.

Goldie turned and said, "It's actually my mother's recipe."

"Then your mother must've been an amazing cook," Rosie said.

"Like mother, like daughter, apparently," Clint said.

They all fell quiet while they continued to eat. By the time Rosie finished and had a second bowl, everyone was gone but Clint and Henry.

As Goldie cleared their bowls away Rosie said, "Goldie, I've misjudged you. When Charlie gets back you and he are going to have to figure out a way to work together."

"In the kitchen?" Goldie asked.

"Yes, in the kitchen."

"Then I don't have to—"

"You still need to learn the business," Rosie cut her off. "I don't want the other girls to think I'm playing favorites."

"I understand."

"Clint," Rosie said, "let's go to the office. You, too, Henry."

They walked down the hall to Rosie's office, where she closed the door and sat behind her desk. Clint and Henry took the two chairs in front of her.

"What's on your mind?" Clint asked her.

"That lawyer, Medford," she said. "Why would someone wanting to buy my place use him to make the offer?"

"Maybe he wanted someone who needed the job and wouldn't ask any questions," Clint said.

"How are we going to find out who his client is?" she asked.

"Henry's going to Kentucky Street tomorrow morning and see if he can follow Medford."

"Why not tonight?" she asked.

"We're hoping he won't go til morning," Clint said. "He assumed I'd be following him."

"And why would he think you wouldn't follow him in the morning?" Rosie asked.

"Hopefully," Clint said, "he'll be looking for me."

"And he won't see Henry?"

"He won't see me," Henry said.

"But . . . no offense, Henry . . . you kind of stand out," she said.

Henry, with no expression on his face, repeated, "He won't see me."

"I hope not," she said. "I want to get this over with so we can go back to work."

"So do I," Clint said.

"And I want Charlie back," Henry said.

"So do I," Rosie said.

"If he wakes up, he might be able to identify one or more of the attackers," Clint said.

"*When* he wakes up," Henry said.

"Right," Clint said, "when." He looked at Rosie. "Are you going to open again tonight?"

"Not if you say no."

"Then no."

"What about tomorrow?" she asked.

"I think not until we find out who wants to buy you out or drive you out."

"And hopefully Henry will find that out tomorrow," she said.

Clint looked at Henry. "You better turn in. You want to be on the street early tomorrow."

"I do not sleep much, but you are right. I will rest my body."

Without another word he stood and left the office.

***

Clint and Rosie discussed other possible moves to make, but in the end came back to their original plan.

"Hopefully," she said. "Henry comes back with an answer. You should turn in also, Clint. Unlike Henry, you do need sleep."

"What about you?"

"I always have paperwork," she said. "I should only be another hour."

"All right, then," Clint said. "I'll see you in the morning."

Clint left Rosie's office, didn't run into anyone else on the way to the stairs. He went up to the hall, walked to the room Rosie had given him. He was about to open the door when he saw the light beneath it. Someone was inside. He felt fairly certain it had to be someone from inside the house. Just to be on the safe side, he kept his gun hand ready as he opened the door.

The person responsible for the light was seated on the bed, her hands clasped in her lap.

"Don't shoot," Goldie said.

Chapter Thirty

Clint entered the room, closed the door and turned to look at her. She stared back at him meekly.

"What's going on, Goldie?"

She shrugged and looked embarrassed. She was wearing a robe and, when she pulled it tightly around her, it became obvious she was wearing nothing underneath.

"You heard what Rosie said about my cooking," Goldie said.

"Yes," Clint said, "she said it was delicious,"

"She said she was going to let me cook with Charlie. But she also said I was going to have to learn the business so the other girls wouldn't think she was playing favorites."

Clint suddenly remembered Rosie saying she wished she had a man who could break Goldie in.

"Goldie, did Rosie send you here?"

"No!" Goldie said, quickly. "N-no, this was my idea."

"And what idea is that?" Clint asked.

"I need you, Clint," she said. Slowly, she started to pull the robe down from her pale, smooth shoulders.

"Now wait a minute—"

"Rosie always said she'd have someone break me in," Goldie continued. "I decided I want that to be you." Another tug and the robe slid down further, exposing her firm, peach-sized breasts. "I need you to show me."

"Goldie," he said, "you need some sleep. This can wait—"

"Wait until when?" she asked. "There's nothin' else goin' on, right now. Everyone else is asleep."

She stood up and allowed the robe to fall around her ankles. She had a lovely, perfectly formed body for her five-foot-five frame.

"Goldie," he said, "we'd have to be quiet."

"I can be quiet," she said.

"I hope so," Clint said. "One thing we don't know is how you'll react to intense pleasure."

She cocked her head to one side and gave that some thought.

"I don't think I've ever known intense pleasure," she said. "This'll be interestin'."

Clint walked past her, removed his gunbelt and hung it on the bedpost. Then he turned, started to unbutton his shirt, but stopped.

"Let's be sure about this, Goldie," he said. He knew he could put her robe back on her and shove her out into the hall, but at some point a man was going to—as she and Rosie put it—break her in. It might as well be a man who would be concerned about hurting her.

"I'm sure, Clint," she said. "I'm sure you'll be gentle, and I'll learn all I need to learn."

"As long as you're sure," he told her. "We can stop any time you want."

"Let's start with you getting' undressed," she said. "Unless you're shy."

He smiled at her and continued unbuttoning his shirt. After he peeled it off, he sat on the bed to remove his boots.

"Let me help."

Before he could stop her, she stepped over, put her back to him, bent over and grabbed his boots. Her bare behind was a glorious sight that his body began to react to.

When his boots were off she turned, got down on her knees, and began to undo his trousers.

"Goldie—"

"Some of the girls talk about how much they enjoy undressing a man. I'm beginning to see why they like it."

When she got his pants undone, he lifted his hips so she could draw them off. Then she carefully slid her fingers into the waist of his underwear and pulled them down. When she got them past his thighs, his erection popped out and startled her.

"Oh!" she said, and then "Oh, my." She rocked back on her heels and stared. She covered her mouth, and then looked at his face. "Oh, I'm sorry."

"Don't be sorry," he said. "Take your time and look at it all you want."

She seemed reluctant, but then stared openly.

"I never expected—" she said, then stopped.

"What?" he asked.

"Well . . . Ella said that men's . . . peter were big, ugly, veiny things. But you . . . you're so smooth and . . . well, pretty."

"I'm sure some men are . . . ugly. You see, they—we—don't all look alike."

She remained back on her heels and stared at his face.

"You've done this before."

"Done what?"

"You know . . . broken girls in."

"I don't call it that. But yes, I've been with girls who are having sex for the first time."

"And you've taught them?"

"I suppose you could say that."

"And have they all been . . . well, young."

"Well, not all," he said.

"But they've all been virgins."

"Not all," he said, again. "Some of them were just . . . inexperienced. Some have been mothers who only had sex with their husbands in order to have children. They never thought of sex as enjoyable."

"But you showed them."

"Yes."

She put one hand on each of his thighs and gripped them tightly.

"Then show me."

Chapter Thirty-One

Clint allowed Goldie to familiarize herself with his erect penis. She touched it, stroked it, squeezed it, asked questions about it. Eventually she asked a question he knew would come up.

"I've heard some of the girls talking about men's . . .manhood being different sizes. They say some are too small and some are too big." She slid her hand up and down his shaft and asked, "Which is yours? Have you seen other men's?"

"I have seen other men's . . . manhood. There are many names for it, but let's go with manhood."

"How did you see them? Why? When?"

"Mostly during the war. I saw enough to form an opinion about whether mine is small, medium, or large. In my opinion, mine is among the largest I've ever seen."

"Good!" she said, seeming relieved. "I was hoping I wouldn't have to deal with any, uh, bigger."

She wrapped both hands around his hard cock—by now all of her handling of it had brought it completely erect—and asked another question.

"Some of the girls—mostly Ella—talk about taking a man's manhood into their mouths. They say men like when a woman does this. Do you like it?"

Clint had decided he was going to have to be completely honest with Goldie.

"Yes, I do, very much."

"Do you expect a woman to do this?"

"I don't," he said. "I leave it up to the woman."

"But," she released it from one hand, but held on with the other, and asked, "How do I get this into my mouth? I mean, how much of it goes in?"

"You have to find that out for yourself," he said. "It'll be up to you whether you like it or not. Some women try wetting it first."

"Wetting it . . . how?"

"With their tongue."

"You mean . . . spittin' on it?"

"No, not spitting," he said, "just . . . licking it."

"You mean . . . tasting it?"

"Well, yes, you could call it that."

She opened her hand so she could look at him.

"Startin' where?"

"Some women start at the bottom and lick upward," he said. "Others wet the top, and when it's very wet they slide it into their mouth."

"But . . . how much of it goes into the mouth?"

"That's different for all women," Clint said "Some take it in a little at a time, try to accommodate as much as they can. Others open their mouths and take it in as quickly and deeply as they can, and then begin to suck it."

"B-but how does it fit?" she asked.

"I think you might have to ask some of the other girls about that," he said. "I think we'd better deal with the, uh, act of having sex."

"You mean, putting it in me?"

"Yes, that's what I mean."

"But . . . isn't it too big?"

"Again," Clint said, "we have to deal with . . . wetness. When you get wet down there, it slides in more easily."

"How do we get me wet?"

"Touch yourself down there, Goldie."

"T-touch myself?" she asked.

"Yes, very lightly."

She put her hand between her legs very slowly, then pulled it back.

"Oh!" she said. "I'm already wet."

"That's because you're excited."

"I am?"

"Take my word for it," he said. "You are." And look here, a man can get you wet with his hand, before trying to enter you."

"Show me."

"All right, but let's lie down on the bed first."

"Together?"

"Yes," he said, "side-by-side."

When she was on her back, he started touching her breasts first, so that her nipples became turgid. He explained this was another reaction to being excited.

"Do you feel that?" he asked, rubbing his palm over her nipples.

"Oh! Yes, I feel it."

"Now we'll go lower," he said, gliding his hand down over her abdomen, until it was between her legs.

"Now," he said, "tell me when you feel something."

He delved into her pubic hair with his fingertips until he found the slick, wet lips of her vagina. He stroked them, causing her body to jerk.

"I feel that!" she whispered.

"Okay," he said, "Now I'm going to try something else."

Very slowly, he inserted his middle finger into her vagina and wriggled it.

"Oh," she said, "I definitely feel that!"

Chapter Thirty-Two

As it turned out, Goldie truly enjoyed the pleasure Clint showed her sex could be. She managed to suck his penis fairly comfortably after a few attempts, and eventually settled comfortably on her back with her legs spread wide so he could easily slide into her. Once he was inside her wet warmth, moving in and out of her, she managed to match his rhythm, comfortably.

After several hours they laid together, side-by-side, and talked.

"I think you got the hang of this fairly quickly," he said.

"Do you think so?" she asked. "I could stay longer for more lessons."

"I think it's time for you to go back to your own room and get some sleep," Clint said "Remember, everyone expects you to make breakfast."

"Clint, is it always as good as it was tonight?" she asked.

"It depends on the people involved," Clint said. "I'm sure you've heard some horror stories from the other girls."

"Oh yes," she said. "Ella likes to tell stories. I just don't know if they're all true. I get the feelin' she just doesn't like men."

"Some men just want a quick in-and-out," he explained. "And some of them are brutal. I think men coming to a whorehouse are not looking for much beyond the physical act."

"Do you treat all your women the way you treated me? So gently?"

"Again, that's up to them," he said. "Some women want it quick and rough, others want it slow and gentle. I try to give them what they wanted." Briefly, he thought of his time with Julie's mother. He thought he had given her mother just what she wanted, which included staying away from the young girl.

"You better get dressed now," he said.

Reluctantly, she stood up and put her robe back on.

"Let me check the hall," she said. "I don't want anyone knowing I was in here."

Clint hadn't been sure Goldie was telling the truth about not being sent to his room by Rosie. Now it seemed that was, indeed, the truth.

"I'll see you in the mornin'," she said to him. "Thank you for this."

"You're welcome, Goldie," he said.

She paused before leaving.

"Did you experience any real pleasure, Clint?" she asked him.

"I guarantee you, I did, Goldie. Good night."

She smiled and slipped into the hall.

***

It seemed apparent that none of the girls knew what had gone on between him and Goldie. When Clint got to the kitchen, Goldie was already at the stove.

Several of the girls—including Ella—were already seated at the table, eating.

"Clint," Goldie said, "Good morning. Full breakfast?"

"Very full."

"Comin' up."

She brought him a plate brimming with scrambled eggs, meat, potatoes, and flapjacks.

"Thank you," he said. "Did Henry have breakfast?"

"Yes," she said, "he was up very early, and I made sure he ate before he went out."

That satisfied Clint and he started to eat. Some of the girls left while others came in. Ella stayed and, eventually, Rosie came in. Goldie gave her a plate almost as loaded as Clint's. Rosie sat right next to Clint, and they talked while they ate.

"Did Henry get out early?" she asked.

"He did."

"Good," she said. "Let's hope he comes back with something."

Clint pushed his empty plate away. Rosie looked across the table at Ella, who had finished eating but was still there.

"Ella, I want you on the door today."

"What? That's Goldie's job," Ella complained.

"Goldie's got kitchen duty today. I want you on the door. With a gun."

"Rosie—"

"Just do it! Tell anybody who asks that we're not opening today. If anyone gets aggressive, use your gun."

"I've never shot anyone before."

"Clint gave us all lessons," Rosie said. "I have confidence in you."

Ella hesitated, trying to think of a way out, then gave in, stood and rushed from the kitchen.

"Thanks, Rosie," Goldie said.

"This is only until Charlie comes back," Rosie told her. "Get this place cleaned up and plan dinner."

"Yes, ma'am."

"Clint?" Rosie said and left the kitchen with Clint right behind her.

When they got to the front of the house, Ella was already standing by the door with a Colt Peacemaker in her hands.

Chapter Thirty-Three

Rosie led Clint to her office. They sat across from each other.

"I need Henry to come back with some information," she said. "I'm getting tired of waiting for this to be over. I want us to *make* it be over."

"So do I," Clint said. "I've got other things to do."

"I know," she said. "I'm taking up your time, too."

"If I didn't want to help you, Rosie, I wouldn't."

"This waiting has to end, Clint, so we can all go back to our lives."

There was a knock on the door.

"Come!" Rosie said.

The door opened and Ella stuck her head in.

"Ella! You're supposed to be on the front door."

"There's someone here to see you," Ella said. "I thought you'd be interested."

"Who is it?" Rosie asked.

Ella pushed the door open, and Clint saw a huge, hulking figure enter. He looked like Henry Moon, only a foot taller.

"Charlie!" Rosie cried.

She jumped up from her desk, ran around and threw her arms around the big Indian.

"Are you supposed to be on your feet?" Clint asked.

Charlie looked at him and Rosie said, "Charlie, this is Clint Adams. He's trying to help us find out who did this to you . . . to us. He's right, should you be up?"

"I woke up and knew you needed me," Charlie Moon said. He looked pale, and still had a bandage around his head.

"Henry's helping, too," Rosie said. "You should go back to the doc's."

"I ain't leavin' here," Charlie said.

"Okay, then," Rosie said, "come on, I'm putting you in your own bed."

"Where is Henry?"

"He's trying to find out who hired a lawyer who came to make an offer."

"What lawyer?"

"Come on," she said, "I'll tell you on the way to your room."

Clint walked with Rosie and Charlie as far as the stairs, then stopped.

"You put him to bed," he said to Rosie. "I'm going to see if I can find Henry. Meanwhile, see what you can find out from Charlie. Maybe he recognized some of the men that injured him."

"All right," she said, "but be careful."

Ella opened the front door for him and said, "Watch your back."

"You, too," he said. "Keep that gun handy, but don't shoot unless you have to."

***

First Clint went to Kentucky Street to check the lawyer's office. He found it locked, but the front door was flimsy. When no one answered his knocking a second time, he put his shoulder to the door and forced it.

Next, he let himself into Medford's office and started going through his files. He had two file cabinets. One was empty, and the second was more than half empty. Most of Medford's file seemed to be stuffed into one drawer.

Clint assumed that when he was hired to make an offer to Rosie, he would have started a file. Whatever his client was planning, Clint was fairly sure Medford was kept mostly in the dark. As he went through the files, he found that most of Medford's work involved making offers to buy out businesses. He didn't find a file for The Doll House, but in most of the files he found the client with the name Helen Dexter.

Chapter Thirty-Four

An hour earlier Louis Medford had sat across the desk from his client, Helen Dexter, in her office at the hotel.

"What did she say when you made the offer?" she asked.

"She never let me get that far," Medford said.

"You didn't tell her how much it was?"

"She wouldn't hear it."

"Louis—"

"I know, I know," Medford said. "You're disappointed."

"I'm more than disappointed," Helen said. "I don't want to get overly aggressive."

"Didn't that happen when your men sent that big Indian to the doctor's office with a busted skull?"

"We don't know how badly hurt he was," Helen said, "but that was his own doing."

"And you lost two men to the Gunsmith."

"How was I to know he'd get involved?" Helen said. She sat back in her chair and thought a moment. "Okay, we've got to send the boys in again. You said Adams followed you from the house to your office, yesterday?"

"That's right."

"Did he follow you here this morning?"

"I don't think so."

"You better hope he didn't," she said. "I don't want him finding out that I was behind the attack on the house, and on that little slut, Reed. When you leave here, make sure you go out the back way."

"That's the way I came in, and that's how I'll go out," Medford said.

"Good," she said. "Make damn sure nobody's following you. Then I want you to find our new friend and have him come see me."

"Why use him when you have your own local men?" Medford asked.

"I want someone unknown, and a real professional."

"He's a professional, all right," Medford said, "A professional killer."

"Whatever he is, I intend to use him to get what I want," Helen said. "If you don't want to help me, I'll get someone else."

"No, no" Medford said. "I'm in. I'll get him here."

"Good," she said. "Then get out."

"Yes, ma'am."

Medford left the office and made his way to the back door. Julie, who didn't like the man, saw him leave and went to her mother's office.

"Mother, why was that horrible man here?"

"Nothing for you to worry about, dear," Helen said. "He's just handling a business matter for me."

"What kind of business?"

"The kind you have no reason to know about," Helen said. "Aren't you supposed to be on the desk?"

"Yes, but—"

"Just go and do your job, Julie," Helen said. "You don't need to be involved in anything else."

Julie turned and headed for the door, but stopped before leaving.

"Mother, have you seen Clint Adams? Has he checked out?"

"As far as I know, he still has his room."

"Then where is he?"

"I don't know," Helen said, "and you shouldn't be concerned. As far as we know he could be involved with that young floozy who runs the whorehouse."

"Why would he do that?" Julie wondered.

"I don't know, but apparently he killed two men for her."

"The way I heard it, he saved her from being hurt by two men," Julie said.

"Nobody knows what really happened, dear," Helen said, "and it's none of our concern. You need to stay away from a man like Clint Adams."

"But mother—"

"Go back to work, Julie!"

"Yes, mother."

As Julie left the office and closed the door, Helen sat back in her chair. She knew for certain that Clint Adams was helping Rosie Lee Reed, but she hoped he would tire of the task and give it up. If he didn't, she was going to have to hire more men to help her accomplish her goals. But first she would have to see what this new man would bring to the table.

***

Louis Medford slipped out the back door of the hotel, looked around carefully to be sure he wasn't being followed, and then made his way along the back to an alley that would take him to the street. He then made his way back to Kentucky Street, but not to his office. Instead, he went to a saloon on that street called The Dead Man's Hand. Over the door was a crude drawing of a pair of Aces and Eights. Inside, over the bar, was a painting of the hand Wild Bill Hickok had been holding when he was shot in the back and killed. This was where he hoped to find the man Helen Dexter wanted to hire, because this was where men like him spent their time when they were in town.

***

Henry Moon managed to follow Louis Medford from his office to the Alabaman Hotel. He watched the man enter and exit through the back door, which he felt certain was an indication that he didn't want to be seen there.

He then followed Medford back to Kentucky Street and saw him enter the saloon. He didn't follow him in because he knew the kind of place it was. They wouldn't serve drinks to Indians, and the clientele would certainly not approve of his presence there.

However, he was able to watch from the window as Medford approached the rough looking individual who was sitting alone. Henry saw the lawyer sit with the man, but then three men approached the saloon but stopping to glare at Henry. The Indian walked away to avoid a confrontation. He felt he had seen enough to satisfy Clint Adams.

The Dead Man's Hand Saloon was certainly the place a person would go to find men who would do anything for money, including busting up The Doll House, and attacking Rosie Lee Reed on the street. Finding out anything further would be for Clint Adams to do.

Chapter Thirty-Five

After searching Louis Medford's office, Clint couldn't find Henry anywhere in town, so he decided to return to the house.

"That was fast," Ella said, when she let him in.

"I found out what I needed to know. Did Henry get back, yet?"

"Not yet."

"Rosie in her office?"

"Yes. What did you find—" she started, but he set off down the hall.

The door was closed so he knocked.

He heard her usual, "Come!"

He opened the door, entered and closed it again.

"That was fast," Rosie echoed Ella's greeting.

"I didn't see Henry, but I got into Medford's office."

"What did you find out?"

"He doesn't have a lot of clients, but he has one I recognized."

"Who?"

"Helen Dexter."

Rosie made a face.

"That stuck-up bitch who owns the Alabaman?" she said, with distaste.

"That's the one," Clint said. "What's she got against you?"

"I have no idea," Rosie said. "I've had very little to do with her, although I've seen her around town. And what I've heard about her is that she has her fingers in lots of pies."

"Heard from who?"

"The men who come here to The Doll House like to poke and talk. The girls relay the information to me."

"Any specifics about what she's doing?"

"No, but maybe now we know. She wants to take over The Doll House, but why? To operate it or shut it down?"

"What did Charlie come up with?"

"Nothing, so far," she said. "He's resting. Maybe when he wakes up, he'll remember something."

There was a knock on the door, and it opened before Rosie could say anything. Henry stuck his head in.

"Henry, you're back!" Rosie said. "Get in here."

He came in and closed the door.

"Whiskey?" she asked.

"Yes."

She poured him one and he knocked it back.

"Another?"

"No."

"You got something?" Clint asked.

"I followed the lawyer," Henry said. "Guess where he went."

"The Alabaman Hotel?" Clint asked.

Henry stared at him.

"If you knew this, what was I doing out there?"

"I went looking for you this morning," Clint said. "I broke into Medford's office and looked at his files. I found Helen Dexter's name in there. I'm surprised, but I'm assuming she's behind all this."

"Well, I have something else."

"What is it?"

From the hotel the lawyer went to the Dead Man's Hand Saloon."

"Where's that?" Clint asked.

"It's on Kentucky street, several streets from his office," Henry said.

"What's the significance of that?" Clint asked.

"That's the saloon most of the troublemakers in town go to," Henry said. "I couldn't go inside, because they don't like Indians there. But I did look in the window and saw the lawyer sit with a man."

"One man, alone?"

Henry nodded.

"Did you know him?"

"I've never seen him before. He is a big man with a wild mane of red hair. And usually all you whites look alike to me, but this man is very ugly."

"Red hair, big and ugly?"

"Does that mean something to you?" Rosie asked.

"Yes," Clint said, "it means I've found Del Thaxton."

***

Clint talked more about Thaxton than he had since arriving.

"If you're after him, why would he stop here in Clanton?"

"He doesn't know I'm after him," Clint explained. "He knows a posse won't leave Kansas."

"So he believes he is clear," Henry said.

"Yes," Clint said. "That's why I'll be able to surprise him."

"But why is a man like that connected to Helen Dexter?" Rosie asked.

"Because she obviously believes she needs a man like him," Clint said. "The seven she's already sent didn't get the job done."

"Why would one man succeed where seven failed?" Rosie Lee asked.

"Because he will do what they wouldn't," Henry said.

"What's that?"

Henry looked at Clint, and when Clint nodded said, "He will kill."

Chapter Thirty-Six

"By the way," Rosie said to Henry, "Charlie's back."

"Where is he?"

"In his room, resting."

"That's what you meant by when he wakes up, maybe he'll know something."

"The doctor told him he'll be fine, but he's still feeling a little muddled," Rosie said. "He should be sharper when he wakes up. And he'll have Goldie to help him with his work here."

"And now we have both of you, me, and the girls to fight off another attack."

"From one man?" Rosie said.

"No," Clint said, "whatever Thaxton plans, he's going to have to use locals."

"Why don't you just kill him?" Henry asked. "Find him and kill him."

"If I end up killing him, it'll be his choice," Clint said. "I don't just walk up to someone and kill him."

"Your reputation—"

"—was given to me by others. I don't claim it."

"Why don't we go to the top?" Rosie said. "I can go right up to Helen Dexter and tell her we know it's her."

"That's not a bad idea," Clint said. "But if we do that, I think I should go and talk to her."

"Whether you lay claim to your reputation or not," Rosie Lee said, "that might be the way to go."

"Thaxton won't allow her to give up just because it's me," Clint said. "And I don't think she would, anyway. I'd like to find out why she's doing this, what's behind it. That might help us put a stop to it."

"And then what?" Rosie asked.

"And then I take Thaxton back to Kansas to stand trial," Clint explained.

"And?" Rosie asked.

"They'll hang him."

"You hope."

"No," Clint said, "they'll definitely hang him for multiple murders."

"Unless you end up killing him on the way back," Henry pointed out. "He won't go quietly."

"Like I said," Clint replied. "It'll be his choice."

***

When Henry left Rosie's office he decided to go up-stairs and look in on his cousin, Charlie.

"Well," Rosie said, "seems like we found out quite a bit."

"And our two problems have become one and the same," Clint added. "It looks like I'll have to deal with Thaxton, and Helen Dexter, to get this all resolved."

"You stayed in her hotel for a short time," Rosie said.

"In fact," Clint said, "I'm still checked in there."

"Did you get to know her, at all?" she asked.

"Slightly," Clint said. "But, I spent more time talking to her daughter, Julie."

"Now there's a sweet, clean young thing," Rosie said.

"You and she are actually the same age," Clint said. "You're just a lot more mature."

"I had to grow up a lot faster and learn to take care of myself," Rosie pointed out. "She's had a mother taking care of her for her whole life."

"Her mother might become as notorious as yours," Clint said.

"For her sake, I hope not," Rosie said. "So how do you want to play this?"

"I think I should go and see Helen Dexter first," Clint said. "Maybe I can convince her to stand down and call off whatever she's planning."

"By scaring her?"

"By reasoning with her."

"And what if she's unreasonable?" Rosie asked.

"Then my next step is to lock up Del Thaxton so he can't work for her. Without his expertise, she might change her mind."

"Lock him up where?" Rosie asked. "In Sheriff Poole's jail? I don't think he'd be real helpful with that. In case you haven't noticed, he's not much of a law-man."

"I don't need him," Clint said. "I just need his jail."

***

When the big, ugly, red-haired man entered the hotel lobby earlier that morning, Julie got a chill just looking at him.

"Well," he said, as he reached the desk, "what a cute little thing you are."

"C-can I help you, sir?"

"And polite," Thaxton said. "I like that."

Julie stared at the man.

"I need to talk with your mother, little girl," he said.

"What? Why? What has my mother—"

"She sent for me," he said, cutting her off.

"What?" Julie asked. "What for?"

"That's what I'm here to find out," Thaxton said. "Why don't you go and tell her I'm here."

"Does she know you?"

"Tell her Louis Medford sent me."

"Just a minute."

Julie rushed down the hall to her mother's office and opened the door.

"Mother, the most horrible man just came into the hotel. He says you sent for him."

"Did he give his name?" Helen asked.

"No, but he said Louis Medford sent him."

"Ah," Helen said, "all right, bring him back—no, on second thought." She stood up. "I'll come out and get him myself."

She came around the desk toward her daughter, but Julie didn't move.

"Mother," she said, "what does he want?"

"Julie," Helen said, "don't worry about a thing. This man is going to do a job for me."

"Mother—"

"Honey," Helen said, patting Julie's shoulder, "you have to mind your own business."

She turned her daughter around and pushed her into the hall ahead of her.

Chapter Thirty-Seven

It was midday when Clint left The Doll House and walked to the Alabaman Hotel.

"Clint!" Julie cried out, when she saw him enter. She ran out from behind the desk and stopped short of hugging him.

"Where've you been?"

"I'm sorry, Julie," he said. "I've been a little busy."

"Helping Rosie Lee Reed, or finding your man?"

"A little bit of both, actually. Is your mother around? I need to speak with her."

"She's in her office," Julie said. "Come on, I'll walk you back there."

Julie led Clint down the hall and opened the door to her mother's office without knocking. Helen looked up from her desk.

"Julie," she said. "What's wrong? Why aren't you on the desk?"

"Somebody's here to see you mother," Julie said, and stepped aside.

"Who—" Helen started, but then Clint stepped into the room.

"I told Julie I needed to talk to you," he said. "She was kind enough to walk me back."

"I see," Helen said. "Well then, I suppose you better have a seat. Julie, go back to the front desk."

Julie tugged on Clint's arm and said, "Don't leave without saying goodbye."

"Bet on it," Clint said.

He sat across from Helen as Julie left the room and closed the door.

"What's on your mind, Clint?" Helen said. "You haven't been around. I was wondering if you had run out on your bill."

"I doubt that was what you were wondering, Helen," he said.

"What do you mean?"

"I know what you've been up to," he said.

"Oh? And what's that?"

"Attacking the Doll House, and Rosie Lee Reed."

"That disgusting place?" Helen asked. "Why would I attack it?"

"That's what I came here to ask you," Clint said. "What's behind all this?"

Helen sat back in her chair and stared at Clint. He decided to let her think about her answer for a little while. But he finally had to give her a nudge.

"Come on, Helen," he said. "I know what's been going on. You sent those men to trash the house and hurt Rosie Lee. I also know that you're now hiring Del Thaxton to continue the attack. And that you sent the lawyer,

Medford, to make an offer to buy Rosie out. I just need you to tell me why."

"And why do you think I would tell you my business, Clint?" she asked. "Because we spent one night together? You must think quite a bit of yourself."

"That's got nothing to do with this," he said. "I don't want to see anyone else get hurt."

"Oh please," Helen said, "a bunch of dirty whores and an equally dirty Indian?"

"And your hands are totally clean."

"Look," Helen said, "I'm doing this for Julie, and for this town—you know what? Get out of my office. I'm not talking to you about this, anymore."

"I've got one last thing to tell you," Clint said. "If you've hired a man named Del Thaxton to take this over for you, you've made a bad mistake. I'm going to take him into custody and return to Kansas with him, where he'll hang."

"Yes, well, you're assuming I've hired such a man, which I'm not admitting to. Now, please leave!"

"I warned you, Helen. If anyone comes after that house or the people in it, they'll have to go through me."

"Mr. Adams," she said, "while you're here I'd like you to collect your things and check out of my hotel."

"Gladly!"

Chapter Thirty-Eight

When Clint came down from his room carrying his saddlebags and rifle, Julie looked at him in surprise.

"You're leaving?" she asked, as he reached the desk.

"At your mother's insistence," he said.

"What's going on?" she asked. "First this big, ugly man comes here—"

"What? When?"

"No more than an hour ago," she answered. "Apparently, he's now working for my mother, but doing what, I don't know. And now you're leaving."

"I'm leaving the hotel, not town," Clint said. "I still have much to do."

"Where will you be staying? At that whorehouse?"

"Yes," Clint said. "As long as those girls are in danger."

"And who are they in danger from?"

He didn't answer.

"Wait . . . my mother?"

"She's the one trying to buy Rosie Lee out," Clint said, "but I don't know why."

"And the red-haired man?"

"That's Del Thaxton, the man I tracked here."

"Are you going to kill him?"

"As I've told others, that's going to be his choice. I plan on taking him back to Kansas to hang."

"How will you find him?"

"Well, I could just wait for him to find me," he said, "but I think I know where I can find him. It'll depend on how many men he's gathered, by now."

"Don't you have someone you can ask for help?"

"I do have a couple of men, yeah," he said. "And Rosie herself is pretty tough."

"I wish I was tough," she said, "then I could help you as well."

"That would mean possibly going against your mother, Julie," he pointed out. "I would never ask you to do that."

"Then I'll have to stay here and wait to see what happens," she said, glumly. "I'll just have to hope it's not bad news."

"You can help me with something now, Julie," he said.

"What's that?"

"Let me have my bill."

She smiled, "I tore that up a long time ago."

***

Clint left the Alabaman and brought his things back to The Doll House.

"Movin' in?" Ella asked with a smile, as she let him in. He saw that she was holding a gun down in the frills of her skirt.

"Just til this is all over," he said.

"Maybe," she said, "when this is all over, we can get to know each other better. I'm the oldest, you know."

"How old would that be?"

"I'm twenty-two."

"Ancient," Clint said, and grinned to take any sting out of the word.

Clint brought his things up to his room and saw Henry coming out of a room further along.

"Henry," he called.

The Indian turned, saw him coming down the hall, and waited.

"How's Charlie?" he asked.

"He's alert," Henry said. "He's already gone downstairs. He's in the kitchen, but he's got a gun tucked into his belt."

"I saw Ella at the door, and she had a gun in her hands."

"Then we are ready," Henry said. They walked downstairs and Clint told him about his conversation with Helen Dexter. "So we know who is behind all this, but not why," Henry observed. "Do you think we'll ever know?"

"That's hard to say," Clint said. "she's pretty close-mouthed."

"Do we really have to worry about this Thaxton?" Henry asked,

"He's a killer," Clint said, "and she already has five men working for her. All Thaxton has to do is bring the killer out in them."

"Well, you won't have to worry about my cousin and me. I have always had a killer instinct, and Charlie will never let himself take another beating."

"I'd like to face Thaxton away from here, so none of the girls get hurt," Clint said.

"Maybe you can get to him before he puts together any kind of gang."

"I'm guessing he's already done that with the men Helen had hired, plus whatever men he collected from The Dead Man's Hand Saloon."

"If he is looking for killers—and from what you say about him, he is—The Dead Man's Hand is the place to do that."

Clint saw that the front sitting room was empty. He waved at Ella, then he and Henry walked to the kitchen.

Chapter Thirty-Nine

Charlie Moon and Goldie were standing at the stove, side-by-side.

"What's cooking?" Clint asked. "Smells good."

Goldie turned and smiled at him.

"Charlie's showing me how to make an omelet," she said.

Clint wondered where the Indian had learned how to make omelets.

Charlie looked at Clint and his cousin and said, "Sit." Clint and Henry sat at the table. It wasn't mealtime, so the girls were probably up in their rooms.

Quickly, Charlie put a plate in front of each man. A fluffy omelet covered each plate, with peppers, onions, spinach and potatoes all mixed together.

"Wow, this looks good," Clint said.

He and Henry dug in while Charlie and Goldie watched.

"How is it?" Goldie asked, excitedly.

"It's great," Clint said.

Henry nodded and kept eating.

"I'm going to make it tomorrow morning for everyone," Goldie said.

Charlie put the wooden spoon he was holding down and said, "I'm going to check on Ella."

As he left the kitchen Goldie asked, "Can I get you anything else?"

"Coffee would be nice," Clint said.

Quickly, Goldie poured them each a mug.

"I'm going to see what the other girls are doing," she said.

"Do me a favor," Clint said. "Send Charlie back in."

"Sure."

She went off down the hall and in moments Charlie reappeared.

"Goldie said you wanted to see me," the big Indian said.

"Get some coffee and have a seat."

Charlie poured himself a mug and sat across from Clint and Henry.

"How's your head?" Clint asked.

"Sore, but better," Charlie said.

"I meant your thoughts, your memories. We need to know if you recognized any of the men who broke in here."

"One," Charlie said. "His name's Ozzie Gifford. He came in first because I knew him. The others filed in behind him. Before I knew it, they were all on me. That is the last thing I remember until I woke up in the doctor's surgery. He told me what happened and how long I had been there. He wanted me to stay, but I came back here."

"Okay," Clint said," so Ozzie Gifford broke in with four others. Why didn't they kill you?"

"I don't know about the others, but Gifford's a hard case, not a killer."

"So maybe the others aren't, either," Clint said. He told Charlie that Helen Dexter was behind the attack. "She might be used to violence, but not killing. Thaxton is. If he takes the lead how hard would it be for him to turn Gifford into a killer?"

"Ozzie is a follower, not a leader," Charlie said.

"The same may be true of the other four," Clint said.

"And they might recruit more," Henry said. "That means we have to be ready to kill."

"Agreed," Clint said, "if it comes to that. Charlie?"

"I won't take another beating," Charlie said. "I will kill first."

"That's what Henry said about you, which means you need to be armed at all times."

"I have a shotgun in my room," Charlie said.

"Good," Clint said, "carry it with you at all times."

"Right. What are we going to do now, just wait?"

"No," Clint said, "I've already talked with Helen Dexter, but she wouldn't bend. That means I have to go out and grab Thaxton before he gets prepared."

"And what about us?" Henry asked.

"I think the two of you should stay here and be ready in case they try another frontal attack."

"What if you find Thaxton, and he's got men with him?"

"Killing is not my first option, but I have no trouble doing it if I have to."

***

Clint left the two cousins going upstairs to get their weapons. He went to the front door, where Ella was still holding the fort.

"Anybody come to the door?" he asked.

"No," she said. "The word seems to have gone out that we're closed."

"Where's Rosie?"

"I'm not sure, either in her office or her room."

"When you see her, tell her I went out to try and find Del Thaxton. Tell her Charlie and Henry are here and prepared to do whatever they must to defend this place."

"You're going out alone?" she asked.

"Yes."

"Is that smart?"

He hesitated a moment, and then said, "Probably not."

Chapter Forty

Clint went to Kentucky Street and found The Dead Man's Hand Saloon. He stood in front and stared at the faded sign over the door. He didn't appreciate the saloon being named after the poker hand his friend, Wild Bill Hickok, was holding when he was shot to death by the coward Jack McCall. Under normal circumstances he never would have entered the place. But if he wanted to put a stop to whatever Del Thaxton was planning for Helen Dexter, he had no choice.

He went through the batwing doors and stopped just inside. There were men standing at the bar, and sitting at tables, but none of them were Del Thaxton. He walked to the bar and faced the rumpled looking bartender.

"What'll ya have?" the man asked.

"Nothing here," Clint said.

"What's wrong with my place?" the bartender asked. "Not good enough for ya?"

"Not even if you washed the glasses in steaming hot water," Clint said.

"Then whataya want?"

"I'm looking for Del Thaxton."

"Don't know 'im"

"A big, ugly fella with red hair."

The bartender hesitated just long enough to give himself away as he lied, "Never seen 'im. Are you law?"

"No."

"Some kinda bounty hunter?"

"My name's Clint Adams."

The bartender looked shocked.

"Oh, hey . . . uh, Mister Adams, sorry, I didn't recognize ya. What's the Gunsmith want here?"

"I told you, Del Thaxton."

"Well, there was a fella in here recently who looked like that, but he ain't been here since yesterday."

"Okay, then," Clint said, "let's try Ozzie GIFFORD."

"Ozzie?" The bartender looked surprised again. "Whataya want with Ozzie?"

"I understand he's working with Thaxton. I want them both."

"Uh, well, they was sittin' together for a while yesterday but—"

"With who else?"

"Who else?"

"Come on," Clint said, "there's got to be at least six of them, counting Thaxton."

The other men who had been standing at the bar moved away when Clint introduced himself. Now some of them slipped out the door. The men seated at tables were listening to the conversation, but they didn't move. Clint turned and looked at them.

"Is GIFFORD here?" Clint turned and asked the bartender.

"Uh, no, he ain't."

"What about friends of his?"

"Ozzie ain't got many friends."

Clint turned back to the room.

"Does anyone here know a man named Del Thaxton?" he asked.

Heads turned as the men exchanged glances that seemed confused.

"All right, who knows Ozzie Gifford?"

No reply, but the bartender spoke up.

"This fella is Clint Adams, the Gunsmith," he said. "If I was you, I'd answer his questions."

"Who knows Ozzie?" Clint asked, again.

Half the room raised their hands.

"Does anyone know where I can find him now?"

Nobody answered.

"Okay, so quite a few of you know him. How many of you count him as a friend?"

No one answered.

"How many of you have worked with him?"

A couple of men raised their hands.

"Recently?" Clint asked.

One man raised his hand.

"What was the job?" Clint asked.

The man didn't reply, so Clint walked up close to him.

"Um, well—" the man started.

"Let me help," Clint said. "Did you break into the whorehouse, bust up some furniture, knock the girls around and beat down Charlie Moon?"

"Um, well . . . yeah."

"Who else did that?"

"There was a couple of men at the bar when you walked in. They left."

"Have any of you been recruited by Del Thaxton?"

The man didn't answer and look confused.

"What's your name?" Clint asked.

"Waylon."

"Thaxton is a big, ugly, red-haired man."

"Then yeah," Waylon said, "he's been lookin' for men."

"Did he recruit you?"

"No."

"Why not?"

"I don't like him," Waylon said.

"What about the rest of you?"

"I don't know about Jim and Tad—two of the men who left when you came in—but he got Ozzie."

"Where are Thaxton and Ozzie now?"

"I dunno, but I think they're probably lookin' for more men."

"Waylon," Clint said, putting his hand on the man's shoulder, "let's go for a walk."

Chapter Forty-One

Clint pulled Waylon from the chair and walked him outside where it was almost dusk.

"Where're we goin'?" Waylon whined.

"We're going to find Thaxton or Ozzie."

"How we gonna do that?"

"There must be some other places in town like The Dead Man's Hand. Where would they be?"

"Well, there's a coupla places . . ."

"Pick the nearest one and let's start there."

Waylon pointed and said, "At the farthest end of Kentucky Street."

"Lead on," Clint said.

They turned left and continued on Kentucky Street, it went for two blocks and then came to a dead end. From there they could turn left or right, but directly in front of them was a place called The Dead End Saloon.

"Why do all these saloons start with the word 'dead?' " Clint wondered aloud.

"This is the place," Waylon said, "but it's even worse than The Dead Man's Hand. Even I wouldn't drink anything here."

"But it's a good place to recruit men?"

"The worst kind."

"Then let's go."

"Hey, Mr. Adams, I brought you here. Can't I go?"

"Not til we find Thaxton or Ozzie. Go." He pushed the man through the batwing doors. His abrupt entrance attracted the attention of the men standing at the bar and seated at tables.

As soon as the big bartender saw them, he reached beneath the bar and came out with a double-barreled shotgun. It was noisy in the place, but they could hear the bartender clearly as he pointed the gun at them.

"Waylon! I told you the next time I saw you I'd blow your head off!"

"Whoa, whoa!" Waylon cried, holding both hands out in front of him. "This wasn't my idea." He pointed. "This is Clint Adams. He made me come here."

The bartender immediately recognized the name.

"Clint Adams? The Gunsmith?"

"That's right," Waylon said. "You wanna blow his head off?"

Several men laughed and one man called out, "Yeah, Leo, go ahead, blow the Gunsmith's head off!"

That made more men laugh, but the bartender scowled and said, "Shut the hell up!"

Suddenly, it got very quiet, and everyone's attention was on the bartender, Waylon and Clint.

The bartender lowered the barrel of the shotgun.

"Let's lower that barrel a little more before some-body gets hurt," Clint said. "And I'm talking about you, Leo."

As if the shotgun had suddenly become a snake, the bartender set it down on the bar and raised his hands.

"Okay, friend, okay," the bartender said.

Clint decided to have his say right at the door.

"Is Ozzie here?" he asked Waylon.

"No."

Clint didn't see Thaxton.

"Has anybody seen Ozzie Gifford today?" he asked, aloud.

"Yeah," the bartender said, "Ozzie was in here ear-lier."

"Who was he with?" Clint asked.

"A big guy, real ugly, with lots of red hair."

"When they left, did anyone go with them?"

"Yeah, two other men. The big guy said he was hirin'."

"So, when they left there were four?"

"That's right," the barkeep said, and several other men in the place nodded.

"Where'd they go from here?"

The bartender shrugged.

"I dunno."

"Where would they go if they were still recruiting?" Clint asked.

"I'd guess The Last Stand Saloon. It's at the far end of town."

"I'll take you there," Waylon said.

"Anybody else got some suggestions?" Clint asked the room.

There was a lot of head shaking and somebody said, "That sounds like the place."

"Okay," Clint said to Waylon, "let's go."

Outside Clint asked Waylon, "What'd you do to that bartender?"

"I don't really know," Waylon said. "I musta been drunk when I did it, 'cause I can't remember."

"How far is The Last Stand from here?" Clint asked.

"It's a pretty long walk," Waylon said. "We can stop for a drink along the way."

"So another bartender can blow your head off?" Clint said. "I don't think so."

"Trust me," Waylon said, "you ain't gonna want a drink at The Last Stand."

"That's okay," Clint said. "Let's go."

Along the way Waylon asked, "You gonna kill Ozzie and this big fella?"

"That's going to be up to them."

Chapter Forty-Two

When they left Kentucky Street, they walked through several nicer parts of town, then they came to a rundown section with many boarded-up or burnt storefronts. Finally, they came to The Last Stand Saloon, which actually looked like one of the better buildings in the area.

"Looks like they fixed it up some," Waylon said.

"When was the last time you were here?" Clint asked.

"Geez, gotta be a while."

"Anybody going to try to blow your head off?" Clint asked.

"Well, let's find out."

Nobody paid them any mind as they entered. The place was bigger and louder than The Dead Man's Hand Saloon was. There was no point in shouting from the door, so Clint gave Waylon a shove toward the bar.

A saloon girl walked past them carrying a tray of drinks. She had a tear in the thigh of each of her fishnet stockings.

When they got to the bar, they had to elbow their way in. A frail looking bartender came over and asked, "What'll ya have?"

"Some information," Clint said.

"I pour drinks, friend," the barman said. "Ain't got no information."

"Let's try a few questions and see," Clint said.

"I don't think so," the bartender said, reaching beneath the bar. Before he realized what happened, he was looking down the barrel of Clint's gun, inches from his face.

"If your hand doesn't come up empty," Clint said, "it'll be the final bad decision of your life."

It got quiet at the bar as the customers there backed away until Clint and the bartender were isolated. The silence spread through the entire place.

"Now I know whatever you've got down there can shoot right through the bar, but you'll be dead before you know what happened."

The bartender frowned and asked, "Who are you?"

Waylon came forward, said to the bartender, "He's the Gunsmith," and backed away.

The bartender suddenly became very cooperative.

"Okay, okay," he said, "I'm bringin' my hand out."

He withdrew his hand from beneath the bar and wriggled his fingers to show that his hand was empty.

"Whataya need?" he asked, his eyes riveted to the barrel of Clint's gun.

"I'm looking for two men," Clint said, "a big red-haired man named Thaxton, and Ozzie Gifford."

"They was here, but they left."

"How many men were there, total?"

"Four came in," the bartender said. "When they left, they was eight."

"Where were they going?"

"I dunno," the barman said. "I couldn't hear 'em. They was sittin' across the room."

"Did your girl bring them drinks?"

"Yeah, she did."

"Call her over here."

"Ruby!" the man shouted and waved at her.

"What's wrong, Eddie?" she asked, coming over.

"I'm tryin' to keep this man from blowin' my head off."

"What's that got to do with me?"

"Tell 'im what he wants to know."

Little-by-little conversations around the room resumed. Many of the patrons no longer seemed interested in what was happening at the bar.

"What about those days off you said I couldn't have, Eddie?" she asked.

"Yeah, yeah, you got 'em," Eddie said, "just tell this man what he wants to know."

She looked at Clint and smiled, revealing one front tooth missing from a once pretty now ravaged face—which was a shame, because she didn't seem to be thirty yet.

"Four men came in here together, one of them was a big, ugly red-haired fella. You remember them?"

"Sure, I couldn't miss 'em. One of 'em was Ozzie Gifford."

"Did you hear anything they were saying while you served them drinks?"

"Sure," she said. "The big, ugly guy was doin' all the talkin'. By the time he was done there was eight of 'em."

"What happened next?" Clint asked.

"They all got up and followed the one guy out."

"Did you hear them say where they were going?"

"The big guy mentioned The Alabaman. That's a ritzy hotel across—"

"I know what that is," Clint said. "Anything else?"

"Well," she said, and paused.

Clint cocked the hammer on his gun. Eddie's eyes popped and said, "Ruby!"

"The big fella mentioned The Doll House. You know what that is?" she asked.

174

"Yes, I know."

"I tried to get a job there once," she said. "They said I was too old. Hell, I'm only twenty-four now."

"What'd he say?"

She shrugged.

"Somethin' about either tearin' it down or blowin' it up."

Chapter Forty-Three

Outside the Last Stand Waylon asked, "Where are we goin' now?"

"I don't care where you go," Clint said. "We're done."

Waylon heaved a sigh of relief.

"Hey," Clint said, as the man hurried away.

Waylon turned and looked as if he was expecting to be shot. He even put his hands out to shield himself.

"If I find out you warned Ozzie, or Thaxton, about me, I'll hunt you down."

"Don't worry about me, Mr. Adams," Waylon said, "I'm gonna get me a bottle, find a hole and pull it in after me. I ain't comin' out until I heard you left town."

"You're smarter than I thought."

Waylon threw him a salute and ran off down the street to find his hole.

Clint had two choices: go back to The Doll House or go to the Alabaman. Going to the Alabaman might put him up against eight men by himself. He wasn't worried about the seven locals Thaxton may have recruited, but if he couldn't give Thaxton all of his attention, he might be in trouble. The man was a stone-cold killer, and Clint knew he would need to concentrate on him.

If he went back to The Doll House, he would at least have Charlie and Henry Moon to back his play. Not to mention Ella and some of the girls who could at least shoot, to provide some cover.

He decided on The Doll House. That was the place it all started after all.

When Ella opened the door for him, he immediately asked, "Everything all right?"

"So far."

She opened the door wide to allow him to enter. As he did, he saw Rosie coming down the hall.

"Get everybody into the sitting room," he told her. "Where are Charlie and Henry?"

"Charlie's in the kitchen," she said. "I'm not sure where Henry is."

"I'll find him!" he snapped, heading for the kitchen.

As he entered, Charlie turned from the stove. His shotgun was lying within easy reach.

"Where's Henry?"

"He went out back," Charlie said. "You want me to get 'im?"

"I'll do that," Clint said. "You go to the sitting room with your shotgun and stay with the girls til I get there."

"Right."

Clint left the kitchen, went to the back door and stepped outside. There was a barn where Rosie kept a surrey and a few horses. Henry was on the side of the barn. When Clint reached him, he saw that a circle had been drawn on the wall of the barn. There were several knives and a tomahawk stuck right in the center, even though it was dark. Henry was about to throw another knife when Clint called out to him.

"Henry!"

The Indian froze and looked at him.

"Everybody's in the sitting room waiting for us," Clint said.

"Something is happenin'?"

"I'll tell you inside. Collect your cutlery and come on."

Clint ran back to the house. He could hear Henry running behind him. When he reached the sitting room, everyone was there, and Henry came in behind him.

He explained what he had found out and when he was done Rosie said, "Eight men?"

"At least."

The girls all looked at each other, but Ella said, "We can handle 'em."

"Damn right we can," Goldie said.

"That's the way to think," Clint said.

"Do you think they're comin' tonight?" Rosie asked.

"I don't know," Clint answered, "but we're going to be ready for them, tonight, tomorrow or the next day."

"What about the Alabaman?" one of the girls asked. "Maybe you can find them there."

"I don't think Helen Dexter is going to want any shoot outs near her hotel," Clint said.

"I agree," Rosie said. "She'll have it all done here."

"Why don't we do the same thing to her hotel?" Ella said. "Bust in and shoot it up."

"There are innocent guests there," Clint said, "and her daughter knows nothing about all this."

"Clint's right," Rosie said. "This is our business. Nobody innocent should get hurt."

"I think we're all pretty innocent," one girl said, and a few others nodded.

Rosie put her hands on her hips and addressed everyone.

"We all live and work here," she said, "but anyone who doesn't want any part of this can pack up and leave now, no bad feelings. Just let me know and I'll pay you what's coming to you."

She studied the faces of each girl in turn, but no one stepped up.

"All right then," she turned to Clint, "what are we going to do now?"

Chapter Forty-Four

Clint placed Charlie Moon in the sitting room with two of the girls. He told Henry to cover the back with two other girls. Ella remained on the front door, Rosie in her office. Clint reserved the right to move around, but spent most of the night with Ella on the front door.

"What about me?" Goldie asked. "If they come, I want to fight, too."

"Stay in the office with Rosie, Goldie," Clint told her.

"Do you think she has to take care of me?" Goldie demanded.

"Actually," Clint said, "I was counting on you to take care of her."

"Oh," Goldie said, meekly. "All right."

They stayed in their places all night, and when the sun came up, Clint went to Rosie's office and stuck his head in. Rosie lifted her head off the desk, where she had been asleep. Goldie turned in her chair and looked at Clint.

"Have you been awake all night?" he asked her.

"I tried to stay awake, but I dozed off from time to time," she said.

"Do you think you can get some breakfast together for us?" he asked.

"Sure, I can," she said standing.

"Then get to it, girl," he said.

"Yessir." She hurried out past him, into the hall and to the kitchen.

"Are we giving up?" Rosie said.

"The fact that they didn't come after us last night means they'll probably be coming today," he said. "I just want everyone well fed, because we're all going to be tired."

"Good thinking," Rosie said.

"How are you feeling?" Clint asked.

"I'm ready to defend my house, and my business," Rosie said. "I still can't figure what this Dexter woman has against me. She has her own very successful business, and from what I understand, she has others. Why does she want mine?"

"I don't know if we'll ever find out the answer to that question," Clint said. "But we're going to make sure it doesn't happen."

"No matter what we have to do," Rosie added.

"Your girls all stayed," Clint said, "but how many of them do you feel will go as far as they have to go?"

"Ella's ready, and Goldie is committed. For the others, I guess we'll just have to see."

"I'm going to let everyone know they can have breakfast in shifts," Clint said, starting to leave.

"By the way, Clint," Rosie said, "Goldie told me what you did."

"What I did?"

"Breaking her in," Rosie said.

"Oh, that," he said. "I didn't really think of it as 'breaking her in.' But she was bound and determined to learn—"

"I'm not criticizing you," she said. "I appreciate what you did for her, but I'm thinking of keeping her in the kitchen from now on."

"That seems to be where she wants to be," Clint said.

"And as she gets better," Rosie observed, "I may lose her."

"I can see her cooking in her own place in the near future," Clint said.

"I hope that happens for her," Rosie said.

"It would be easier," Clint said, "if she had somebody—like a partner—backing her."

Rosie smiled and said, "That's just what I've been thinking."

***

They all ate Goldie's omelets in shifts, so that some-body was always on the lookout.

"Wow," Rosie said to Clint as they ate side-by-side, "this is amazing."

"Thinking a little more seriously about a partner-ship?" Clint asked.

"You know, I am," Rosie said. "But I won't tell her that for a few years, yet."

When they finished eating, Rosie went back to the office and Clint went to the front door to allow Ella to eat breakfast.

"I'm not that hungry," Ella said. "Let some of the others go first."

Clint passed the word to Henry and a couple of the girls, and then went back to Ella.

"The word seems to have got out that we're not open for business," she said. "No one's come near the door."

"I think when Thaxton decides to make his move," Clint said, "they'll come *through* the door."

***

Thaxton stopped his men before they turned the cor-ner and came within sight of the house.

"Ozzie, you take three men and hit the front door," he said. "Once you're inside, kill anythin' that moves."

"Kill?" one of the other men said.

"Is that a problem?" Thaxton demanded. "You're gettin'paid enough for this job. And if we kill everyone, there won't be anyone to identify you."

"What about Adams?" Ozzie asked.

"Who?"

"Clint Adams."

"The Gunsmith?" Thaxton asked. "What about him?"

"Well . . . he's in there."

"That's crazy," Thaxton said. "What would the Gunsmith be doin' here?"

"Didn't you hear he was in town?"

"I did but I didn't believe it." Thaxton thought if the rumor was true, Helen Dexter would have told him. If he had to face the Gunsmith, it was going to cost her more. And she would have to explain why she didn't warn him.

"Change of plan," Thaxton said. "Ozzie, take three men and go in the back. I'll take the front."

"Right."

"And nobody take on the Gunsmith," Thaxton said. "He's for me."

"You can take him?" Ozzie asked.

"Gifford," Thaxton said, "I can take anybody."

Chapter Forty-Five

"Clint!" Ella shouted from the door. "They're comin', and fast."

Clint had been sitting on the stairs. Now he jumped up. "Lock the door! It should hold for a few minutes."

One of the girls who was watching the back door with Henry came running down the hall.

"They're comin!" she shouted.

"Go to the kitchen, get Charlie and take him to the back door!" Clint snapped at her. "That door won't hold after one good charge."

The girl ran to the kitchen, then to the back door with Charlie behind her, shotgun in hand.

Clint turned to face the front door.

"Ella, stand next to me."

She moved so that they were facing the door side-by-side. That's when they heard the splintering of wood and Charlie's shotgun from the back.

There was a crash from the front door, but it held.

***

When the front door didn't give the first time, Thaxton backed off. He figured if the Gunsmith was inside, when the door did give, they would be facing his gun. He decided he didn't like that. He wanted to face Adams on his own terms. He quickly forgot all about what Helen Dexter wanted him to do. He wanted the Gunsmith.

As his men hit the door again, he turned and ran, heading for the Alabaman.

***

Without Thaxton, Ozzie and the six men were easy pickings. There were shouts of pain from the back, as the front door came off its hinges. The three men stumbled in, guns in hand, but they were off balance and not prepared for Clint's gun.

Ella fired her weapon, and several girls fired from the entrance of the sitting room. They didn't hit anything, but the sound of their guns at least contributed noise.

It was Clint's gun that was extremely accurate. The three men stumbled through the doorway but had to do so one-by-one. If they had been able to come in fanned out, it might have been more difficult.

As it was, Clint's initial shot struck the first stumbling man in the top of his head, killing him instantly. The other two men tripped over the first man, and Clint calmly shot them both in the chest.

When it fell quiet, three men were stacked in the front doorway like firewood. There was no noise from the back.

"Keep this door covered in case there's more!" he shouted to Ella and the other girls.

He turned and ran to the back. When he reached there, he saw the door on the floor in pieces, but lying on top of the pieces were four men. Two of them had one of Henry's knives in their chests. The other two looked as if they had taken the full brunt of Charlie's shotgun. There was copious amounts of blood splattered everywhere, and two girls had vomited.

"Go get cleaned up," Clint told the girls, who hurried back down the hallway, hands covering their mouths.

Charlie and Henry stood there, stone-faced.

"Good work," Clint said.

"And the front?" Charlie asked.

"Seems quiet," Clint said. "But where's Thaxton?"

"I did not see a red-haired man," Henry said.

"Neither did I," Clint said. "It looks like he sent these men in without him."

"Then where is he?" Charlie asked.

"There's only one place he'd go that I can think of."

"Do you want us to come with you and cover your back?" Henry asked.

"No, stay here and clean up. I don't imagine the sheriff will be along any time soon."

"We will take care of this," Charlie said.

"I'll be back," Clint said.

He stepped over the dead men and out the back door.

***

When Julie saw Thaxton enter the lobby, she grew frightened. As he approached the desk she asked, "Did my mother send for you?"

"I'm not workin' for your mother anymore, girlie," he said. "I've got my own business."

"What—" Julie started, but Thaxton reached out and grabbed her arm. "You're hurting me!"

"I'm just gettin' started, Girlie."

"Let go of my daughter!" Helen Dexter ordered.

Thaxton looked over at Helen, who was pointing a gun at him.

"You're takin' on more than you can handle, lady," Thaxton said.

"I heard there was shooting at the other end of town," Helen said.

"You shoulda told me I'd be goin' up against the Gunsmith," Thaxton said.

"I thought you knew he was looking for you."

"Lookin' for me? For what?"

"He said he tracked you here from Kansas. He intends to take you back to hang."

"What the hell—is he a bounty hunter, now?"

"You should ask him," Helen said. "He's right behind you."

Thaxton turned his head and saw Clint standing in the doorway.

Chapter Forty-Six

Thaxton released Julie's arm. Helen rushed over, put her arm around her daughter and pulled her from behind the desk. Thaxton turned to face Clint.

"What's this all about, Adams?" he asked. "What'd I ever do to you?"

"You killed people in Kansas, Thaxton," Clint said. "One of them was a friend of mine. He was just crossing the street and you shot him down."

"So you followed me here," Thaxton said. "What're you doin' in that whorehouse?"

"Just helping a friend," Clint said. "Turns out my problem and hers crossed paths."

"This bitch is your friend?"

"No," Clint said, "Rosie Lee Reed. She owns The Doll House."

"Well, I ain't got nothin' to do with that, right now."

"No, you don't," Clint said. "You left Ozzie Gifford and your men there to die."

"Too bad," Thaxton said. "But I got a whole new problem now."

"Yeah, I know," Clint said. "Me."

"There's two women in the way, here, Adams," Thaxton said. "You want them to get hurt?"

"They're not between us, Thaxton.

Thaxton sneaked a look behind the desk, and noticed that Julie wasn't there, anymore. He knew he should've held onto her arm. Now she and her mother were off to one side.

"It don't matter," Thaxton said. "You're gonna find out you shouldn't've followed me."

"And you're going to find out you shouldn't've killed a friend of mine."

"I ain't goin' back, Adams," Thaxton said. "Nobody's hangin' me."

"That's your choice, Thaxton," Clint said. "I'd rather take you back then kill you, but . . ." Clint shrugged.

"Any time you're ready, Adams," Thaxton said. "You been around a long time. I always knew I was younger and faster than the Gunsmith. This is my chance to prove it."

***

Helen Dexter was tempted to shoot Thaxton in the back, but the truth was she had never shot anyone. She was also curious enough to see which man was faster.

She kept her gun ready because if Thaxton did outdraw Clint, she just might have to shoot her first man.

"Mother . . ."

"Let's just watch, honey," Helen whispered. "Just watch."

***

Clint knew Thaxton as a bank robber and killer. He had never heard the man called a gunfighter. But Thaxton certainly seemed confident. And he was right about one thing—he was younger, but it remained to be seen if he was faster. Clint always knew he would meet someone faster someday. He had made peace long ago with the eventuality that he would die under somebody's gun.

He studied Thaxton, searching for a tell, a giveaway to when he would make his move.

Thaxton smiled.

"You're lookin' for a tell," he said to Clint. "I ain't got one."

Clint drew and fired, the bullet struck Thaxton in the chest, paralyzing his arms, and he slumped to the floor.

When Clint reached him, he was still alive.

"I only needed a tell," Clint said, crouching over the man, "if I was going to let you draw first."

The light in Thaxton's eyes went out.

Chapter Forty-Seven

Clint stood, holstered his gun, then looked at Helen and Julie Dexter. Julie looked relieved, but Helen was pointing her gun at him and appearing very serious.

"Mother," Julie said, "put that down."

"Quiet, Julie," Helen said. "Clint, drop your gun."

"I don't think so, Helen."

"Don't make me shoot you."

"I'm not," Clint said. "I'm not taking any action against you. Besides, I don't think you would shoot me."

"You've ruined my plans," she said. "I have to start over."

"I think you're done, Helen," Clint said. "Be satisfied with your hotel and whatever other businesses you own. Leave Rosie Lee and her Doll House alone."

"I can't do that. If I leave her be, she'll become as bad as her mother."

"Her mother?" Julie asked. "Who's her mother?"

Helen kept her eyes on Clint but answered her daughter.

"Belle Starr."

"And how do you know that?" Clint asked.

"I knew Belle Starr," Helen said. "She was a real bitch. Twenty years ago she took everything I owned. Now I'm taking everything her daughter owns."

"Belle is still alive," Clint said. "Why not go after her?"

"I am," Helen said. "When I'm finished with her daughter, she'll come for me, and I'll be ready."

"With more men?" Clint asked. "So far you've hired an inferior bunch."

"I'll get better at hiring men," Helen said. "I'll be ready."

"No, mother," Julie said. "I won't let you."

"You can't stop me, Julie."

"I can and I will."

Helen took her eyes off Clint to look at her daughter. Clint knew he could have drawn his gun and fired in that moment, but he didn't. He decided to let Julie have her say.

"What do you think you can do to stop me?" Helen asked her daughter.

"I'll get in your way, Mother," Julie said. "And the only way around me will be to go through me."

Helen looked confused.

"Are you saying the only way I can continue is to kill you?" mother asked daughter.

"That's right, Mother."

"B-but why would you do that?"

"To save you, Mother," Julie said. "To keep you from doing more horrible things."

"Y-you think I'm horrible?"

"No, mother," Julie said. "I think I can keep you from becoming horrible."

Helen stared at her daughter, then looked at Clint and lowered her gun.

"That's some daughter you've got there, Helen," he said.

"Yes," Helen said, "yes, she is."

She turned and the two women embraced.

***

Clint went back to The Doll House to tell Rosie, Charlie, Henry and the girls that it was all over.

Henry and Charlie had loaded the bodies onto a buckboard and taken them to the undertaker.

"The sheriff was here," Rosie said, "but we told him we didn't need him."

"I'll stop at his office on my way out of town and tell him everything," Clint said.

They were in her office, sitting across her desk from each other.

"What about Helen Dexter?" she asked,

"I don't think you'll have to worry about her any-more," Clint said. He didn't bother telling Rosie that Helen Dexter knew she was Belle Starr's daughter. "Her daughter will make sure of that. I think you and Julie have a lot in common."

"Like what?"

"You're both daughters of very strong women."

Chapter Forty-Eight

Clint woke the next morning with a firm, naked butt pressed up against him. He turned his head to look at her and remembered Ella coming into his room in the dark and sliding into bed with him.

"Just a farewell you can remember," she whispered, before sliding on top of him and taking his cock inside her steamy depths, "to show you how the oldest girl delivers."

And she delivered quite nicely. Now he slid out of bed without waking her, got dressed and went downstairs. He found Rosie and Goldie waiting at the bottom of the steps.

"You didn't think we were gonna let you slip out without a good breakfast, didja?" Goldie asked.

They each grabbed an arm and walked him to the kitchen . . .

***

Clint collected his Tobiano from the town livery. He had never really had a chance to move it to the Doll House's barn.

"I know, Toby," Clint said, as the horse ignored him while being saddled, "you're mad at me, but you're going to have a nice run today."

He paid the hostler and rode out of Clanton.

***

He gave the Tobiano a good run for a while, then slowed him down for a spell. He was heading West, but that was as far as he had planned. He could go back to Kansas and report the death of Del Thaxton, but he could also do that with a telegram. He wanted the next stop to be someplace peaceful where he could stay out of trouble, for a while.

He was a few miles out of Clanton when he saw a rider coming toward him on the road, moving at a canter. He reined in to wait.

As the rider came closer, they were dressed like and rode like a man, but he recognized her, and was fairly satisfied that this wasn't more trouble.

When she reached him, she reined in and stared at him.

"Clint Adams?"

"Hello, Belle."

It's been a lot of years for us," she said.

"Yes, it has."

Belle had hardened over the years, but he could still see the young girl he had known years earlier.

"Are you comin' from Clanton?"

"I am."

"I got a daughter there," she said "heard she was havin' some trouble. Thought I'd ride in and give 'er a hand."

"I wouldn't do that, Belle."

Belle frowned.

"Why not? You know 'er?"

"I do, indeed," Clint said. "Why don't we ride some together and I'll tell you a story about a very determined young woman."

Upcoming New Release!

THE GUNSMITH

TO STEAL FROM THE DEAD
BOOK 484

In a town in Kansas, Clint is approached by a woman who claims an undertaker stole her husband's belongings before burying him. Clint discovers this is true, and that the man has done it before. Clint takes on the task of proving the under-taker is crooked and tries to get the belongings back. He finds out the undertaker is not working alone, and proving him guilty won't be easy.

For more information
visit: www.SpeakingVolumes.us

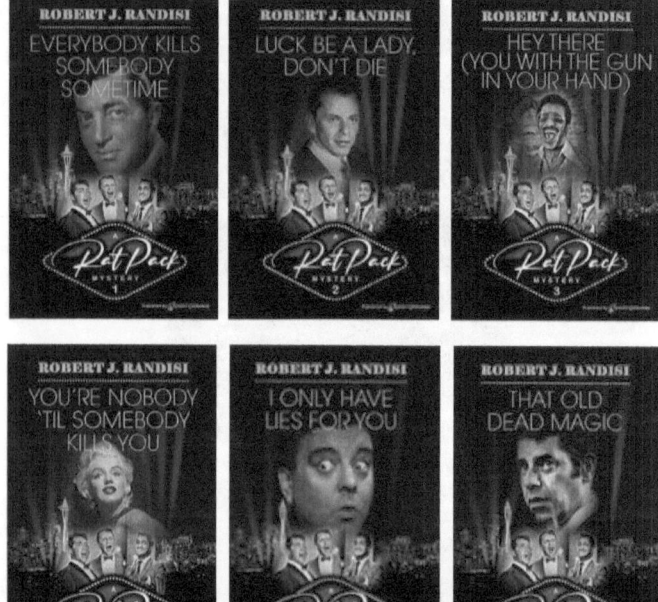

Now Available!

THE GUNSMITH GIANT SERIES

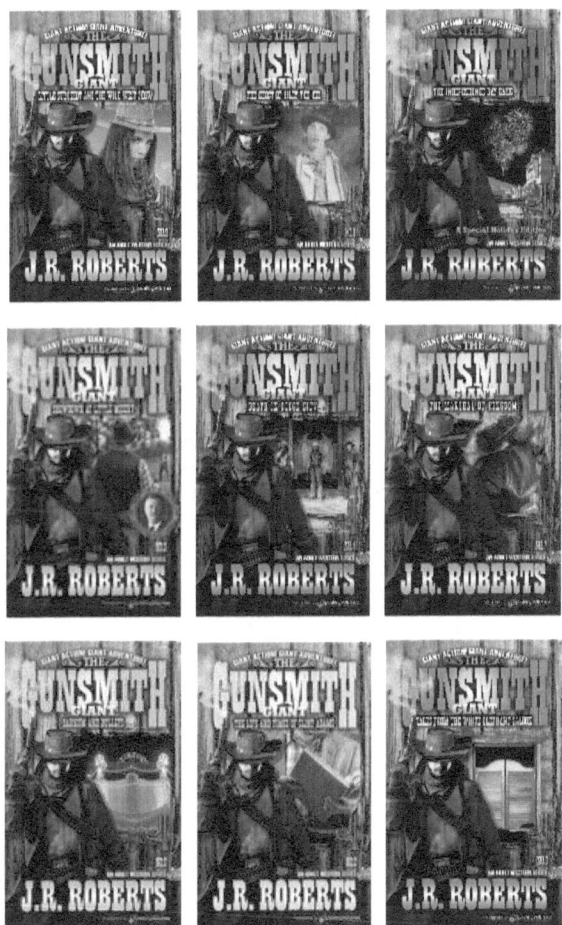

Now Available!

LADY GUNSMITH
BOOKS 1 - 10

For more information
visit: www.SpeakingVolumes.us

Now Available!

AWARD-WINNING AUTHOR
ROBERT J. RANDISI (J.R. ROBERTS)

For more information
visit: www.SpeakingVolumes.us

Now Available!

TALBOT ROPER NOVELS
ROBERT J. RANDISI

For more information
visit: www.SpeakingVolumes.us